HELL'S BACKYARD: THE COMPLETE
CASES OF TUG NORTON, VOLUME 2

HELL'S BACKYARD

THE COMPLETE CASES OF TUG NORTON, VOLUME 2

EDWARD PARRISH WARE

ILLUSTRATIONS BY
F.M. FOLLETT

COVER BY
LEJAREN HILLER

POPULAR PUBLICATIONS · 2023

TABLE OF CONTENTS

HELL'S BACKYARD

Blinkey, Now a Picture of Satan at His Worst,
Wheeled, and I Saw a Knife Flash. Nosey
Connors Had Time for Only a Strangled Cry—

1

BIG JOE DROPS IN

I HAVE SAID before, and I repeat: The sleuth who persists in going around with his holster hitched forward, and his fingers, itching with desire, caressing the butt of his gun, does not last long. Some vengeful gangster bumps him off, or his chief drops him on the skids.

That applies to the regular cop, and even more rigidly to the private agent. Never since I founded and began operating the Kaw Valley Detective Bureau, have I kept an operative one minute after he betrayed a tendency to throw his gun upon any and all occasions where gun-throwing could possibly be done and got away with.

I assert that this business of detecting crime and tracing criminals is better done with the head than the gun—and I invite proof to the contrary.

I'm stressing this antigun attitude of mine because I want it clearly understood. I am, you might say, presenting my alibi in advance. For, in the meanderings of the case I now have in mind, it was on the cards that I was to be picked up bodily, as it were, and flung into the middle of some of the fastest gun-scrapping it has ever been my lot to experience.

Might not such as that be expected to happen in hell's back yard?

I plead, in advance, the circumstance of location, and dire necessity, for deviating from my antigun-throwing rule upon that occasion.

It was Big Joe Murphy who sent his card in to me in Kansas City that day, else I might not have gone prowling in the back yard heretofore alluded to. Joe Murphy, however—well, if you were around Kansas City in the good days about ten years ago, you'll recall the big Irisher who directed traffic at the intersection of Twelfth Street and Grand Avenue.

That Irisher was Big Joe Murphy. He quit the force, though, went to Oklahoma, and prospered most gratifyingly. Then, all at once, the prosperity began to fade—at least, to give notice of fading—and Murphy took train for Kansas City.

So, having been a good pal of Joe's, I couldn't turn the job down. It was out of town, but the pay offered made my eyes bulge—and, as I have said, Big Joe was a mighty good friend of mine.

I had watched the cook eying a tall, filthy bum—
and I was not unprepared for what happened.

"Tug," said Joe, wasting no time in a preamble, "I'm in a hell of a fix—and maybe ye can get me out!"

"Joe," I replied, looking his huge bulk over and noting that he filled my office chair and overflowed on the sides, "tell me how!"

"I'm afther wantin' to be told how, that's why I come to ye, lad!" he exclaimed, wiping his red, perspiring, mournful countenance with a handkerchief. Would I be comin' to ye, or to anny wan else whatever, if I knew how? Would I not be afther doing that little thing for meself? I'm askin' ye!"

"I see the fine Celtic logic of that, Joe," I apologized. "So I'll amend my answer to read: Tell your Uncle Fuller your trouble."

"Ye'll be knowin', I'm thinkin', that I wint to Oklahoma whin I honored th' request av th' chief that time, and quit th' force," Joe began. "At anny rate, so I did. I'd saved a bit of salary—I'd wink whin I spring that one, Tug, only I don't feel like doin' it—and I wint into th' dirt-movin' business. I gyppoed for awhile, meanin' I took subcontracts—"

"Never mind the explanations," I interrupted. "It so happens that I've slung 'a long-line' myself, back in the drear, dead days. Go right on, and don't stop to interpret."

"I'll do that. I made money, lad—a lot of it. Luck broke for me from th' start. Pretty soon I was in shape to handle a big contract for meself. That made me still more money. To-day, the J. Murphy Construction Company is somethin' av an institootion in Oklahoma—also, Texas, Arkansas, and elsewhere.

"Ten months ago, come July next, the Oklahoma and Southern Railroad Company let contracts for constructin' th' roadbed for a fifty-mile branch line. They let it in two sections. Wan begins at Red Rock, on their main line, and extends twenty-five miles east across th' hill's an' hollows which constitoot that part av Oklahoma, to end at Sand Creek. Th' second twenty-five miles begins east av Sand Creek and runs west to it. I got th' first section.

"Now—an' pay attintion to this, Tug me lad—th' company wanted some fast work done on this branch line dump, so they ups an' offers a bonus av fifty thousand dollars for th' contractor who got his section finished first—specifyin' a time limit, av coorse.

"For th' first twenty miles everythin' run along smooth enough—smooth, anny-how, as anny dirt-movin' outfit ever moves. I took an' kept a good lead on Tony Malvern, which got th' contract for th' second section. Thin things begun to happen.

"Accidents—that's what I minded they was at th' first. Me stable tent at me number one camp caught fire wan night—a night of high wind, it was—an' I lost two hundred head av good work-mules, all their gear, a couple thousand dollars' worth of feed, an' a lot av other stuff which I can't recall right now. I had to outfit that camp all new. A week later, me powdershack was blowed plumb to hell, loosin' me another thousand cold, besides killin' two of me men who happened to be comin' past th' place from me number two camp at th' moment.

"Ye'd think, lad, that that would be enough bad luck to happen in wan week. It was—so far as luck was in it. For I know now that luck played no part in thim things at all! Th' very nixt night, about two in th' mornin', a hundred yards of finished dump was blowed up on me. A hundreds yards, mind ye! Clean loss!"

Joe ended his tale of woe there for a moment, and I saw his big face grow hard, and when he raised his eyes to me again there was a glint of steel in them.

"Thin, two nights ago, murder was done," he went on. "Jimmie Doyle, me gineral foreman—th' best dirt man that iver laid a pickhandle over th' head of a fightin' skinner— was knifed in th' back! Damn th' bloody divils that done it! Killed on th' dump, not wan hundred yards from camp! Lad, I'd rather lost me whole outfit, me contract, almost me own life, than had him go that way! As fine a lad as iver walked a dump, was Jimmie Doyle!"

The big man's frame shook, and the look in his eyes was pitiful—though the grief in them was well tempered with rage.

"Of course, you would, Joe," I told him soothingly. "What was the idea for killing Doyle? It's easy to see that Malvern is trying to hold you back, so he can win that bonus. But, in just what way would—"

"What way!" Joe blazed. "Man, had ye known Jimmie

Doyle, little need would ye have to ask that question! Jimmie could get hands, and keep 'em! He could get more good work out av twinty men than anny other boss in Oklahoma could out av fifty! He was a dirt mover from th' ground up! Why, Tug me lad, Jimmie Doyle was th' mainspring of th' whole works! That's why th' murderin' divils got him!"

I nodded, and rage began to tincture my thoughts. Killing a man because he was a good man! A first-class craftsman—loyal and square!

"But couldn't you protect yourself, Joe?" I asked. "Couldn't you have placed the work under guard, and avoided this mischief?"

"Hell! Do ye think I didn't do that same? Av coorse, I did! An' what did it get me? Nothin' at all, at all! How guard aginst a thing that ye can't localize? Tell me that, will ye? All th' approaches to me camps, as well as th' dump itself, has bin watched close—an' th' diviltry has happened just th' same. As for th' county and State officers—but I needn't say anythin' more. Ye'll be knowin' about thim kind yerself!"

"And it's your idea that I can go down there and get the goods on whoever is causing your trouble, eh?" I inquired.

"Exactly. It might be that ye'll be able to sthop it an' save th' day for me," Joe said. "But, more thin all that, I want ye to find th' murderin' divils that boomped off poor Jimmie Doyle—an' thin lave 'em to me! Understhand, Tug—lave 'em to th' two hands of me!"

Joe got up, his big fists clenched, eyes blazing. Grief was gone, and animal rage held him.

I shook my head negatively. "I'll take the job, Joe," I told him. "But when, and if, I lay Doyle's killer by the heels, he'll have to go the law route. No violence on your part—none at all—much as I'd like to back you in such a play. Do you agree to that?"

Joe was silent for a long moment, brooding eyes on the rug. Then he looked up and nodded.

"Have it your way, Tug," he said. "Ye're right, av course—but, God above, lad, ye niver knew Jimmie Doyle!"

2

INNOCENT-LOOKING, BUT—

I SENT JOE away feeling a bit better, and called Jim Steel, my chief assistant, into the office.

"Jim," I said, by way of greeting, what do you know about hell?" Steel looked me over, asked how long I'd been feeling that way, and offered to get a doctor.

"Because," I went on, motioning him to a chair, "I'm going to offer you a chance to brush up on just that locality—or worse. You will join Big Joe Murphy, who just went out, and whom you know very well, at Union Station in one hour. You will accompany Joe to his camp in eastern Oklahoma, and, arriving there, will pose as a detective—"

"Huh?" Steel broke in. "Let me get that again. Pose?"

"Exactly. Let it be widely known that you are down there to detect. Go about it in the regulation fiction-book manner—but don't do any detecting. I mean by that, don't yield to any urge to go out on trails which will take you away from camp after night has fallen. I'm not kidding you, Jim—I'm in dead earnest. After dark, keep close. I take it you think a lot of Jim Steel, and want to preserve him in the service of society as long as possible. Therefore, don't be tempted to do more than pose, as I have instructed."

I related the circumstances which brought Joe to me,

pointing out that the gang after him was absolutely ruthless; that they would get him, Steel, the first opportunity, and think no more of it than they would of killing a crippled mule.

"By posing in camp," I explained, "you will be protecting me, who shall be posing as something else, at the same time. Above all, keep an eye on Big Joe, and if he takes a notion to start any investigating on his own hook, knock him down and hog-tie him.

"He's in greater danger, right now, than he ever has been before in his life—but he doesn't know it, else doesn't give a damn. Watch him. You'll hear from me, when I'm ready. Ever have anything to do with mule skinners?"

"No," Jim replied. "Though I've crossed up with a few of the breed here in Kansas City, when they've been in to blow their stakes. That's about all."

"Humph! Well, you'll be a lot wiser, after a few days. I remember what an old timer told me down in Texas, a good while ago, before I quit chasing cows for a living. I was about to roll my bed and light out for other parts, and he took occasion to offer me a bit of advice. 'Lad, keep away from th' skinner camps,' he told me. 'A big camp, one where mebbe four, five hundred men is hired, ain't exactly hell— it's a few yards farther on. It's hell's back yard.'

"I failed to take his advice, and I learned that he'd expressed it well: Hell's back yard. So that's where you're headed for now, Jim—hell's back yard. Draw from the cashier as you pass out. Notify friends and relatives, if any, where you've banked your savings, and what lawyer has your will. I'll see you within a few days—I hope."

At the door Jim paused, turned and gave me a half serious, half amused, and wholly comical look. "Tug," he said, "just how much damn foolishness have you been feeding me, and just how much—"

I didn't let him finish. "Jim," I broke in, "in all seriousness, you will, within the next few days, be among men who, as a class, are the wildest, most lawless you have ever hooked up with. Not but what there are some fairly decent, self-respecting fellows among them—but, in an overwhelming majority, the first named predominate.

"Be careful. At night, suspect your own shadow. Better yet, don't make any. Stay where there is lots of light—and don't, whatever you do, fool around the outskirts of the camp. Ask Big Joe. He knows."

"Got you!" said Jim, and departed.

Jim gone, I proceeded with my own preparations. First, I visited a second-hand clothing dealer in Fifth Street. There I secured a pair of yellow corduroy pants, somewhat worn, but by no means in a disreputable state; a pair of scuffed but serviceable shoes, a blue cotton shirt, a shiny brown coat and vest—and, lastly, the most important item of all, a high-roller Stetson hat. A hat that had seen service, and been reblocked a time or two.

At another shop I secured a razor, a bar of soap, a pocket mirror, a towel, and a big needle with some thread. Elsewhere I procured two pairs of dice—one pair square and the other as crooked as the devil himself—and a couple of decks of cards which I afterward altered to suit.

A shop which dealt in new but cheap articles of clothing supplied the balance of my outfit. There I bought a pair of cheap socks, a suit of underwear—the dingy, yellow kind which looks as though it has been washed in a muddy creek—and a couple of blue bandanna handkerchiefs.

Every item in the above list was important—so much so that I chose them with all the care of a man who realizes that his life might well depend upon the selections made.

Does that sound melodramatic? It may sound so—but it is the grim truth. For I was headed for the "jungles"—and in the jungles are many different kinds of men, and there most anything can happen.

At a drug store, operated by a very good friend of mine, I made a final purchase. An ounce bottle of white powder— innocent-looking powder. But my druggist friend took a wallop at the Harrison Anti-Narcotic Law when he sold it.

3

INSIDE THE GATE

WHEN I UNLOADED from a "rattler" at Red Rock, two days later, I looked the hobo I pretended to be. The stains and dust of freight train travel were markedly visible. With the high-roller Stetson set well down over my forehead, the brim shading my eyes after the manner of all true mule-skinners, I stood on the little wooden platform above the depot and looked the town over.

There wasn't much to see. Six frame business houses, two of them "drug stores"—the kind that made Oklahoma and Kansas famous—and the other four doing business as dry goods store, grocery, restaurant, and feed store. Fifteen or twenty weathered frame dwellings lay scattered in view.

Beginning at a point just below where I stood, and stretching away through the rocky hills to the east, lay the new railway grade with its twin lines of rusty rails, rusty because as yet unused by trains, and near by stood a new water tank.

Under the tank, resting on the wide timber foundations, I could see a number of men, and toward them I made my way. Getting nearer, I recognized them for what I foresaw they would be: Mule-skinners, mukkers, and construction camp workers of various sorts. I joined them amid a complete silence.

"Murphy hirin' any hands?" I asked casually, after I had found an unoccupied stringer, sat down, and rolled a cigarette.

Nobody answered. I smoked on. Presently:

"What's th' chances for a smoke, bo?" a broken-nose skinner asked, sitting up and addressing me.

I drew out my bag and papers and tendered them— though with no great show of willingness. Rather as though I would, but didn't particularly care to. He rolled a smoke, passed the bag and papers back, took an inhale or two, and spoke:

"Outa Kay-See?"

"Uhuh."

"See Shorty Blake up there?"

"Heard he was doin' a rap for vag, out at Leeds. Don't know anything about it, myself. Bullwhip Kennedy's there, though. Him an' Johnson-bar."

"The hell, they are! Ain't seen Bull ner Johnson-bar since we worked for Joyce, over on th' Santefee double track!"

"They come in off Colter's job, over in North Kay-See."

"Colter hirin'?"

"They come an' go."

"Sure, bein' right handy to th' big town."

I got up, stretched and yawned. "How far to th' jungles?"

"Five miles down th' grade. Say, Sandy, you was askin' about Murphy hirin'. All he can get—yeah. But they ain't stayin'."

"Stomach robbers?"

"No. Chuck's good enough, an' plenty. Payin' good, too. The works is jinxed."

"Besides bein' jinxed, is it boycotted?"

"No—not yet."

"I see. Time to make a road-stake, though?"

"If you hustle. Jughead Jones is stable boss, number one camp."

"Th' hell he is. Ain't seen Jughead since—lemme see— yeah, since Peterson finished that levee job at St. Joe. Guess I'll get along down th' line. Any you fellers headed that- away?"

Silence.

"Well, so long."

After I'd got a dozen or so feet away:

"Hi, Sandy! "

"Nosey" was on his legs, following me. I waited.

"How's th' weather aroun' Kay-See?" he asked with a wink.

"Snowy—when I left."

"Blinkey Joe still peddlin'?"

"Sure. Walk down th' way a bit—I got somethin'."

Nosey took the lead, there and then. Reaching a point where the brush was thick, he fairly trotted to cover.

"God Almighty!" he gasped. "I ain't seen a flake of snow for two days! Big Joe had a gover'ment dick in here, an'— blooey! Gimme, some—quick!"

A moment later:

"A-a-a-h-h-h-h! Damn! Say, bo! Hope I don't sneeze an' lose it! A-a-a-h-h-h-h! Damn! Guess I'm not goin-n-n— Es-s-sc-c-hehe-w-w-w!"

He sneezed—and lost it!

Right there I made a friend. He held the next one.

"Lissen!" he said, eyes now bright and face twitching. "I'll trade you some good info, for another jolt! What say? Will you? Huh?"

"Gimme th' info, an' if it's worth it, why all right."

"Lissen! Tell Jughead you seen Nosey Conners—an' Nosey told you to look him up. Remember, say: 'Nosey told me to look you up.' Get it?"

"Sure."

"Then, if you've got guts an' wanta make some real jack— you'll do a helluva sight better than herdin' Murphy's old skins over th' dump!"

"What's th' grift?"

"I ain't tellin' nothin'! But it's strong stuff—an' damn good pay! Now—do I git it? Huh? Do I? Hurry, bo—"

He got it—and went back toward the water tank, stepping high, and talking to himself.

I picked him for a snowbird the minute I saw him. Had he given me a real steer? Likely enough. That ounce bottle of coke clinched the thing for him. Quite likely, Jughead Jones was using him for the purpose of recruiting some reliable men for a game he was playing—either for himself, or for Malvern. I'd know later, of course.

Meantime I made tracks along the grade. That bunch of coke-heads under the tank would know the minute they laid eyes on Nosey that he'd had a snort or two, and they'd want some. I didn't intend to give them any. I depended on that little phial of white powder, for which my druggist friend took a chance, to ingratiate me into bigger company than that bunch of stew-bums back there.

I paid no attention, therefore, to the chorus of yells back of me:

"Hi, Sandy! Wait a minute, will ya?"

"Hi, Sandy, old-timer! I'm going yore way!"

And other pleas of like nature. They were snow hungry.

Night was beginning to come on when I reached the vicinity of the jungles. Presently the smell of wood smoke warned me that it was near and I paused to make sure the six-gun strapped to my thigh beneath my trousers was still secure, and that I could slip my hand through the slit in my right-hand pocket and get it quick if I needed it.

I'll explain a few things, then maybe you'll more clearly understand that I might well need it.

Mule-skinners are nomads—they do no work but grade camp work, and know no home but the tents and the jungle camps. They make a "stake," go to the nearest big town, blow it for "coke" and "whiteline"—the latter a mixture of alcohol, simple sirup, and water, but mostly alcohol—go back to the work, or hit up some other job, then pull the same stunt over again.

What time they are not working, they live in a camp of their own, generally located near a big grade job, and which is kept going by those who are at work. Those working contribute stew-money" religiously, too—for they will, a bit later on, be residing in the jungles.

Casting bread upon the water so to speak.

But mule-skinners are not the only type inhabiting the jungles. A far more sinister mob gathers there at times. The yegg, the hi-jacker, the peterman, stick-up—in fine, all the dregs of crookdom sooner or later, find it convenient to hide out in some camp or other. Sometimes they work on the grade, for there is no better place to lose oneself than in a big skinner camp, or in the jungle camps thereabouts.

Many a bottle of nitroglycerine—"soup"—is sweated from sticks of dynamite in jungle camps, to later on be used in cracking a box in some near-by town or, perhaps, a distant city. Sometimes even a really big gun—top-notch crook—avails himself of the protection of the jungles when things are too hot for him in better haunts.

All-in-all, the grade camps, and the inevitable jungles, deserve the designation of my old Texas acquaintance—hell's back yard.

I was going into one such jungle camp presently, and in it I might run across some crook or other whom I had had dealings with in the old days on the force in Kansas City. That was the chance—and about the only chance—I was taking. It was chance enough, believe me.

So, making certain that I could make a quick draw if the hue and cry should be raised, I skidded down the side of the dump, crossed the right of way, entered the timber—and stood for a moment with the jungle camp under my eyes.

4

A MAN FROM THE PAST

A COOKING FIRE glowed in a makeshift oven constructed of stones, in the center of a clearing; on the fire were two five-gallon cans which once had contained oil, but now did duty as mulligan pots. Numerous two-gallon sirup cans, salvaged from the grade camp's dump, contained coffee. A great heap of quart cans lay near by, and from those the diners would partake of the mulligan and the coffee.

Scattered about the edge of the clearing, among the short growth oaks, were sleeping hovels constructed with great simplicity—poles laid across forked sticks set in the ground, and covered with brush and bark. Leaves and dry grass spread under this roof served for bedding.

The jungles held about fifty men, although some of them were merely passing through—perhaps a dozen. The others were, however, temporary dwellers there. They were scattered about on the ground in groups of three and four, or singly.

Those in groups were either discussing other jobs and men they had known, shooting dice or playing cards. The "singles" mostly occupied themselves with such homely tasks as sewing on buttons, patching trousers and coats, shaving, washing out clothes, and even half-soling shoes—

for every big jungle has a more or less complete cobbler's outfit.

One bunch of six were gathered beside a distant hut. They were laughing and talking, all at once and in high-pitched tones. That meant that they had a supply of "snow" and were hitting it up. A jungle or a skinner camp without white-line and coke is a sad spectacle.

I entered camp. A few of the loungers looked me over in silence, noted that I had all the earmarks of the clan, and paid no further attention to me. Such is the way in the jungles, when men are continually coming and going. If a man looks like he belongs there, he makes himself at home with no one to question. It is home to such as he.

If he finds acquaintances, as he likely will if he's an old-timer, he consorts with them. If not, he merely waits until some one begins talking to him, then loosens up. A forward "unknown" is in high disfavor in the jungles. As for eating at the general mess, he is welcome even though broke. If, however, he has a few coins and gives the camp cook something toward the next meal, all the better.

A broke man may stay in camp and eat free for a day or two; if he shows unmistakable signs of illness from drink, too much coke, or from any other cause, he is welcome so long as it takes him to get on his feet again. If, however, the moneyless skinner is in good physical shape, he must "throw his feet"—get out and go to work—within a couple of days at the most.

My opportunity to look the gathering over and determine whether I had any acquaintances there would come at mess time; so far I had seen no familiar face.

Sitting down against a tree at one side of the camp, I

took out my needle and thread and sewed a rent in my trouser leg—put there on purpose. After that was done I selected a wash bucket, went to a near-by branch, returned with it filled and sought the cook.

"What's th' chances to heat a little water?" I asked.

He looked me over, seemed satisfied, took the bucket and found a good place for it on the fire. The fire is the chief cook's own particular province, and woe to the man who takes liberties with it.

"Comin' out, or goin' in?" he asked, after the bucket was on the fire.

"Goin' in, Blinkey." The cook had an eye missing, and I knew it was safe to give him that nickname. Just as Nosey had, after glancing at my thatch, known that my moniker would be "Sandy."

"Outa Kay-See?"

"Passed through. Stayed a week and blowed in. Come from th' West—Utah."

"Uhuh. Workin' fer Cameron out there, I reckon?"

"Yeah."

"Gyppo George still walkin'-boss for Cameron?"

"Was when I left. Yeah."

"Busted, I guess?"

I grinned. To have admitted the possession of any money at all, after spending a week in Kansas City, would have been fatal. At least, it would have detracted largely from my standing as one of the craft.

"Three days on skis," I told him. "Then th' snow dried up."

Blinkey grinned appreciatively. "It always does," he

commented. "Snow plentiful in Kay-See though, I reckon, if a guy's got th'jack?"

"You can shore start a storm any day you want, old-timer," I replied, "if you got th'jack. No trouble a-tall."

"Yeah. We'll eat in a few minutes. Your water's hot."

Invited to "scoff," and dismissed in the same breath, I took my bucket and proceeded to wash up. I had passed muster with Blinkey at least, and that meant much. He was in the premier position in the jungles. He was the cook, and the cook is boss.

"Come and get it, skinners!"

The supper call came, and it was answered promptly. Each man took a couple of cans from the pile and, falling into line, walked past the cook and his helpers. After that he fell to and scoffed.

I had noticed the cook eying a tall, filthy bum with a hangdog look, and was not entirely unprepared for what happened when he presented his can. Blinkey had been stirring the mulligan with a long oak ladle, and when the bum came opposite him he helped him to stew—with a stiff whack across the face with the hot ladle.

"Git, ye damned buzzard!" he raged. "You been warned to throw your feet half a dozen times! Git, damn ye!"

The bum dropped his cans, clapped his hands to his scalded face, and, with a yowl of pain, broke from the line. As he passed rapidly toward the timber, an eater would ever and anon cease long enough to give him a paralyzing kick. Thus was he booted clear out of camp.

He was a "jungle-buzzard." A nonworker—a parasite of the camps. For such there is no mercy in the hearts of the regulars.

I found the stew and coffee good—better than any hash-house on earth can put out. Perhaps hunger helped me to that keen appreciation, for I had purposely come to camp half starved.

To have failed to gorge, I being in good condition and not showing a bad "hangover," would have caused comment. I ate my allotment and, at a signal from Blinkey, took on a second helping. That was a mark of favor extended to me.

I had "stood up" with Nosey and Blinkey—thanks to the hour I spent loafing around Koenig's shipping office in Kansas City the day I left. There I mixed with skinners and picked up information that had enabled me to answer questions about various camps and men. My stall about coming from the West would account for me being unknown in the Southwest. I was congratulating myself while I ate.

If the skinner-camp proper is hell's back yard, the jungle-camp is surely the back fence. There one gets all the real news of the work camps, if he knows how to put his ear to the ground. I'd gained my first objective.

"Say, yu! Haven't I seen yu somewhere before?"

I looked up. The speaker most certainly had—but never by word or look did I admit it.

In the tall, rawboned, lean-faced individual who had so summarily interrupted my scoffing, I recognized Long Bill Leeds—a man I'd sent up in Kansas City for ten years!

5

THE ACID TEST

THE CAMP BECAME absolutely silent. All eyes were turned in my direction. No mistaking the challenge in Long Bill Leeds's tones when he put his question to me.

I looked the speaker over from head to feet, took a bite of bread and slowly shook my head from side to side.

"I don't recollect ever havin' seen ya before, bo," I answered. "Course, yu might 'a' seen me. I been around quite a bit."

"Yeah—quite a bit!" was the sarcastic rejoinder. "Live in Kay-See when you're home, don't yu?"

"I ain't answerin' no personal questions," I replied, getting to my feet with a quick motion. I stood fully as high as Long Bill, and had at least an equal amount of brawn. "I done told yu I don't know yu. Whut yu lookin' for—trouble?"

Long Bill's eyes glinted hard into mine, and his strong jaws clamped. I saw a look of indecision flash over his face, then its lines set hard. He stepped a few paces from me, and addressed the crowd which had begun to circle round.

"If this feller ain't a Kay-See cop, then he's a twin brother!" he declared, raising his voice. "If he's a skinner, then I'm th' governor of Oklahoma—an' everybody knows I ain't!"

Silence. Then Blinkey stepped up, his single eye boring into me. "Yu answered up all right, whilst I was talkin' to yu," he said, "Sounded an' looked like a shore enough long-line man—"

"Lissen!" I broke in. "I was skinnin' jugheads when this here long lad was baitin' back doors for his biscuits! Th' big stiff wants to mix with me, seein' I'm new here—an' by God, I'm plumb willin'!"

"Let 'em mix!" somebody bawled.

"Shut up, you!" Blinkey turned on the speaker like a snarling wild eat. Then, no one answering, he turned to Long Bill.

"Whut makes yu think yu know this bird, Bill?" he asked.

"Hell, I don't only think," Bill rasped. "I know! He got me a stretch down to Jeff—an' I ain't forgot it ner him!"

Bill had gone up for cracking a box in the Stock Yards district. Got ten years, and ducked from a convict farm after putting up three of them. He'd been on the dodge, and successfully, for some three years then.

"Whut yu got to say to that, Sandy?" Blinkey demanded, his face darkening and his eye glittering.

"I says that this long feller here is a teetotal damned liar!" I spat. "I don't doubt but whut he got a ten-year rap—he looks like he might of had several of 'em, and ought to have a few more in a row, but he lies when he lays 'em to me! Me a cop! Hell, I got about as much use fer a cop as a mule has fer milk-weed!"

Long Bill's face had the look of blue granite, and his eyes

were twin balls of fire. Yet he held himself from violent action.

"Make him strip, fellers!" he gritted, almost choked. "Search him good an' plenty! Yu'll find somethin' on him as will prove me right—yu can lay to that!"

"Yu willin' to strip?" Blinkey demanded. "Or would yu rather be stripped?"

"I'll strip, and stand a frisk," I replied. "But if they ain't no proof on me—"

I didn't finish in words. I merely gave Long Bill a meaning look—one that the whole camp understood.

I stepped out in the center of the circle where the firelight showed me up distinctly. My hat went to Blinkey, who searched the sweat-band carefully. My coat and vest went the same way. The contents of the pockets were tossed on the ground in a pile, so all might see.

"Here's somethin'," I said, passing a handkerchief-wrapped object to Blinkey. "I want it back, too—see?"

Blinkey stripped the handkerchief away, glanced at what it contained, started, grinned widely—then placed a nearly full bottle of coke with the rest of my things.

There was a distinct stir among the crowd. They drew nearer, and I heard considerable comment exchanged in undertones. A moment before, that gang had been ready and willing to kill me out of hand, and no questions asked. They would have done so with no compunction whatever.

They still would do so, if convinced in the end that I was what Long Bill accused me of being. But that bottle of coke, with some of it gone and which they naturally supposed I had consumed, was a great item in my favor. It was just what a skinner would be expected to have in his clothes if he had just come out of Kansas City, or any other large center, and had been lucky enough to get out of town with it—kept enough money to buy it for a getaway.

In addition, my clothes looked like I'd lived in them for a long while; they were skinner clothes, to be explicit, and the contents of the pockets were such as any man "on the road" would have. In addition, I hadn't a dime to my name.

Then, dangling my pants in his hands, Blinkey dug up the dice and cards. A close scrutiny of the cards informed him that they were strippers—crooked—and he grinned again.

"Which one of these here pairs of dice is th' ones a feller couldn't throw seven on to save his old gran'mother's life?" he quizzed.

"Th' pair in yore right hand is tops," I grunted. "But yu needn't advertise it!"

The remarkable thing is—at least, it would strike an outsider as being remarkable—that no one took any special note of the holster and gun strapped to my right leg. It was not out of place, and without doubt, there were almost as many guns in camp as there were men present. It would naturally be there.

The gun, crooked cards, crooked dice and the bottle of coke made a deep impression. The tide was beginning to turn in my favor.

"Hell! That ain't no dick! Just a plain, ordinary skinner! A coke-head, an' a crooked gambler. Maybe a gay-cat, too!"

No one expressed the above sentiments, but I knew that such were passing through their minds.

The stripping was over with—even my underwear and socks stood the test. Suppose, now, I'd overlooked a bet, and had on a pair of silk socks, or a suit of linen underwear? I'd have got mine, there and then. And it was:

"Don't find nothin' on him but a lot of proof that he's a skinner," Blinkey announced, his one eye on the bottle of coke, while his tongue began moistening his lips. "Lotta times, Bill, we gits fooled in takin' one feller for another. Course, a dick could a got hisself up thisaway, but not so all-fired complete, I'm thinkin'.

"A dick as has a lotta experience skinnin' jugheads might of figured in a play like this—but it ain't likely. Besides," he paused, then gave out some information, "Big Joe has got th' dick he went to Kay-See fer. Brung him back with him, an' he's at number one camp. He ain't wuth a damn to Joe, I'm hearin'. Just a hick cop, an' he won't last long. Now, I votes this feller Sandy is O.K. Whut you fellers say?"

"By God!" Long Bill yelled. "You're makin' a mistake! He's whut I says he—"

"Shut up!" came a roar from the crowd—and at that instant I did what they expected I would do. I stepped swiftly to Long Bill Leeds, and landed on his jaw.

6

THE BATTLE

WHEN MY FIST cracked on Long Bill's jaw he took a tumble. That didn't spell much, however, for he rolled like a tenpin across the ground, came up standing, and rushed me with all the fury of a rabid dog. I realized that I had a man-size job on my hands—and I knew that my prestige would rise or fall, in accordance with the outcome of the battle.

"Take him, Sandy!"

"Watch him! He's strong for a shiv!" Which meant that Bill would knife me if he could. I was warned.

"Clout him on th' head, an' finish him, Bill!"

"Eat him up, Long Boy!"

Bill had his well-wishers, too.

The battle joined, and raged. I took a clout high up on the left jaw that staggered me, and the next instant got a good one to his wind. Bill grunted, wavered, came on. There was little to choose between us, thus far. We gave and took—and what we gave and what we took was powerful enough to suit fight-fans of the first water.

Once we tangled and went to the ground together, and Bill's grip on my windpipe made me see a deeper night than the moonlit one above us. I broke him away just in time, rolled from him, and staggered to my feet, just as he rushed from a crouch on the ground and swung an upper-cut for my chin. I ducked, and, as he whirled past, caught him under the ear with all I had.

Long Bill plunged on, dropped on his face, his arms crumpling under his weight. He gagged, coughed, struggled manfully to rise—then gave up. There wasn't an ounce of strength left in his body—but there was still plenty of fight there.

I had friends enough then. The victor always has. Blinkey offered a can of cold water, and I drank some, and then bathed my bruises with what was left.

I ached all over. But what mattered it? No doubt there were some men in that camp who were still suspicious of me, but the majority were well satisfied that I was one of them. That's what counted with me—all that counted, just then.

But I wasn't through cementing friendship yet. There was the little bottle of coke—enough to jag up half a dozen. A few words aside with Blinkey, and I knew who to invite to my party. They were the lads who seemed to hold a peculiar sway over the jungles, I called them out.

Yes, I had to take a jolt of the stuff myself—and, wow! It was strong medicine. I don't recommend it. But my new mates had a real enjoyable time—and an empty bottle attested it. I was not sorry to see the coke go; it had served its purpose, and served it well.

Long Bill Leeds, after recovering sufficiently to do so, took himself away. He departed in the general direction of the number one camp of Murphy's, though I suspected there might be other jungles farther off toward the works, and perhaps deeper in the timber. A sort of inner-circle gathering place.

Some such place might well be there, for I was certain that the gang that was doing Big Joe so much dirt had at least a few members scattered in the jungles. It would be much to their advantage to have them there—couldn't hardly get along without them, in fact.

Was Long Bill one of them?

I was ready to bet he was. Bill was not a first class peter-man; he was just a cheap yegg, and often turned his hand at any kind of dirty work offered to him. That he would now make himself scarce I was positive, for he was wanted back in Jeff City, and he'd figure that I would turn him in.

But I hadn't seen the last of Bill Leeds—that I knew just as well as though I could lift the veil and look upon future events.

I slept well that night, in spite of my bruises and the excitement and strain of the afternoon and evening. After breakfast, in spite of Blinkey and his own particular crowd urging me to remain there for a while, I departed for camp number one. Ostensibly, I was going to work. Might do so, in fact, at that. According to what lead I struck that morning, if any at all.

I hadn't forgot Nosey Conners's tip about Jughead Jones, stable boss at number one. There was a chance I might strike just what I was looking for by talking with Jughead. He had some under-cover jobs seeking men, and those under-cover jobs might well be in connection with the dirt being done Joe. I hoped they were.

That Joe was being knifed from inside his own organization was, to my mind, very evident. That would be the best way in which to throw him, and Malvern would probably employ it.

I reckoned that Malvern had a trustworthy lieutenant in Murphy's camp—one whom Murphy also trusted, with less cause to do so. The lieutenant in Joe's employ would have subs here and there, and some of those subs would undoubtedly be keeping a watchful eye on the various jungles.

No doubt Blinkey was drawing pay from the Malvern camp. I couldn't be sure about him, of course, but he'd certainly be in a fine position to serve the cause in the jungles. He would have his eye upon most every man who came in or went out, and he was a case-hardened old sinner for true. In addition, he knew a host of skinners and construction camp workers. By all odds, if Blinkey was not on Malvern's payroll, somebody had overlooked a mighty good bet.

7

I HIRE OUT FOR—WHAT?

TWO MILES FROM the jungles I came to where a big gang was laying steel, and just before I reached them I struck their camp. A good many small tents were scattered about the site, and they were occupied mostly by women. In town they would have been alluded to as "painted women." I don't know as there was much paint in evidence on the faces I saw, but there were other and far more reliable signs which I could read.

An hour later I came to where that hundred yards of finished dump had been blown up. It had been finished, but not yet accepted by the company engineers, so it was up to Big Joe Murphy to rebuild it at his own cost. That was being done.

I did not tarry on the job there, but went on until finally, near noon, I reached camp number one. At that camp four hundred men lived. It looked like the show grounds of a huge circus, so great was the amount of canvas spread.

Below the camp countless teams of mules were crawling about on top of the dump, their drivers manning fresnols, surfacing the finished grade. Everywhere was activity.

I found my way past the huge stable tent and back to the

corral. There I found the tent of the stable boss, Jughead
Jones, and after ten minutes search found the boss himself.

No better description of Jones could be given than this:
He looked very much like a gaunt, gray mule—as much as
a man could look. Hence his nickname of Jughead. A man
about fifty, I judged.

"Well," he said curtly, "what's your trouble?"

"Figured to set in on a job, if so be there's one open," I
told him.

"What's your graft?"

"Oh, I sling a long line sometimes; good stable hand,
and good in a harness room."

"Uhuh. They all say they're good. I've got a job open for
a good harness—"

I gave him a slow wink, and we sauntered away to a
remote corner of the corral.

"Well, what you mean by that wink?" Jughead demanded,
coming to a stand and elevating one foot to the bottom
rail of the fence.

"Nosey Conners," I said slowly, "told me to look you up."

Silence, during which he stared off across the corral as
though interested in anything else under heaven but me.
Then:

"Know Nosey pretty well?"

"Yeah."

"Where at?"

"Around Oklahoma City, Kay-See, St. Joe, and a lotta
other places."

He nodded. "Where you work last?"

"Utah. For Cameron."

"Know th' walking boss out there?"

"Yeah. Gyppo George."

"Where'd you stay last night?"

"In th' jungles, over toward Red Rock."

"Know Blinkey?"

"Sure I know him. We had a session last night—"

"You ain't a coke-head, are you?" he asked quickly.

"Naw! I just brought along a little bit for the boys. Hate th' damned stuff, I do!"

He nodded in a satisfied manner. "I didn't think you looked like a snowbird," he stated. "I reckon I can use you. If you work like you are told, you'll pull down five hundred for a little job which is goin' to be pulled to-morrow night. Go back to Blinkey, and tell him I said to put you on. Just say that: 'Jones said to put me on.' He'll understand. Get it?"

"I shore do. An' I'll work anywhere you put me, though I ain't got no notion what you want me to do," I put out for a feeler.

"That's the kind of men I'm looking for—them that'll work wherever they are put, and ask no questions."

I turned suddenly at sound of footsteps behind, and beheld a squat, heavy-set man of about forty approaching across the lot. He looked like authority, and a black cigar, mark of importance in a skinner-camp, protruded from under a short black mustache.

"Another hand, Jug?" he queried, coming to a stop and sizing me up.

"Yeah, Mike—one for Blinkey."

At that the man called Mike looked at me with new interest. After a bit he nodded and, without further words, went away.

"Who's the gent?" I asked.

Jughead gave me a look full of meaning, then answered:

"He's Murphy's camp boss," he said, "You'll see him later—maybe."

Murphy's camp boss, eh?

Well, it was beginning to look like I'd struck a real lead. One that pointed toward the big gun, and no mistake!

8

"GIT THEM HANDS UP!"

I LEFT CAMP at once, making no attempt to get in touch with Steel or Big Joe. I felt certain that it would have been impossible for me to approach either without that fact being known. Anyhow, there was really no need at the moment for me to do so.

It was fifteen miles back to the jungles, and too much of a walk, on top of the one I'd already made, for me to cover before night. Luckily I caught a lift on a freight wagon which was going to the steelgang camp, and at the camp I fed and loafed until dark.

Rested, I resumed the hike for the jungles. If the job I was hired for was to claim me on the following night, it behooved me to learn as much as I could about it right away.

So far, Tony Malvern's hand was hidden, in so far as bringing the skullduggery directly home to him was concerned. Perhaps he could never be touched, unless his lieutenant, whoever he might be, could be trapped and made to talk.

As for the job I was to participate in, I had good reason to think it was in connection with a final stroke against Murphy. He was within a few miles of Sand Creek, and

Malvern, in spite of the delays he had been able to cause Joe, was still several miles behind in his work. The situation demanded action, and paralyzing action at that, if Malvern was to finger that bonus.

So I hustled on, hoping to be let in on the scheme by Blinkey, and in time to circumvent it. There was a young moon that night, and my path over the cross-ties between the rails presented no difficulties. I would reach the jungles within a couple of hours, and before the gang turned in for the night.

I had been walking for an hour at a pretty fast clip, the roadbed following a rather crooked course along a valley between hills, when I concluded to rest a short while and have a smoke. A big bowlder at the side of the track looked inviting, and I sat on it and loaded a pipe.

Just as I was about to scratch a match I saw someone moving along the dump from the west—a lone man. He came on until almost opposite me, looked about him for a moment, missed me in my position on the bowlder, then plunged down the dump on the far side, crossed the right-of-way, and disappeared in the timber.

He had hardly gotten well away when a second figure appeared, halted at the same point, then followed the first into the woods. Then came a third and a fourth—all single, and all following the same path into the timber.

I waited, refraining from lighting the match, watchful. Then a fifth man appeared from down the track, and the moonlight disclosed his identity. It was Long Bill Leeds. A moment, and he too took the path through the timber.

"Something going on over there somewhere!" I assured

myself. "Probably that second jungle I have been thinking about—the inner-circle gathering place."

I waited for fifteen minutes longer, and no one else came. Then I crossed the right-of-way and slipped off through the woods on the trail of Bill. Bill was a yegg, his specialty being old-fashioned safes in small towns—ones he could crack with a bit of "soup and soap," since the more modern ones in the big towns were beyond his limited skill.

It was possible that the retreat for which he and the others were then headed was a rendezvous of a private character; which he and his "mob" used. If so, it was unlikely that I would gain any information about Malvern and his plans. On the other hand, it might well be a gathering place for the gang working for Malvern. It was worth investigating, at any rate.

There was a faint footpath which I had some difficulty in following, and it led straight back between steep ridges which were clothed with post-oak and black-jack trees, the undergrowth being quite heavy. Needless to say, I moved with utmost caution, not knowing at what moment I might round a turn of the trail and find myself altogether too close to my quarry.

Long Bill Leeds was cagey—cagier than I had given him credit for. Quite likely he had brought up the rear of his party in order to do just what he did—hide beside the trail and make certain no one was following.

At any rate, that is just what he did.

"Git them hands up! Quick!"

9

A RUNNING FIGHT

THE COMMAND CAME in low tones, but it was none the less menacing for that—and Bill Leeds's six-gun looked ugly in the moonlight.

I had walked into a trap!

While following the footpath I had slipped my gun out of its holster, and was carrying it in my right hand, down against my leg—but Long Bill's weapon was within three feet of my head. He had but to thumb the hammer, and I'd pass out.

Still, that was just what would happen to me anyhow. Death was awaiting me a bit farther along the path, and maybe not an instantaneous one either. Should I submit, and me with a gun in my hand?

"Oh, it's you, is it?" Bill snarled. "Caught spying, eh, Mr. Cop Norton? Git 'em up, damn yu—"

I got one up—the right one—and with speed. So quickly, and so unexpectedly, that Bill Leeds was out before he knew his danger. His gun exploded, of course, since his thumb was holding the hammer back at the moment, but simultaneously with the report of my weapon, I dropped to the ground, and the bullet he had released lodged in the hillside beyond.

I didn't wait to examine him. A man doesn't live long after a forty-five caliber slug has passed clear through his stomach, and I had great need for hurrying. Those two gunshots would bring the rest of the crowd, and bring them in a swarm.

I started on the back track, ran perhaps a hundred feet, then stopped in full flight. A gun flashed in the darkness beyond, and a bullet hummed over my head so close I fancied I felt the heat as it passed.

I turned back, ran swiftly past the spot where Bill Leeds lay, and on between the ridges, eyes probing here and there in the hope of finding a point of easy access to the top on one side or the other.

I could, of course, have ducked into the brush, but that would have got me nowhere. I would have been hemmed in surely, I thought, and my capture assured.

Beyond me the ridges stretched, apparently without a break. They were steep, with outcroppings of ledge rock, and along the tops there was scarcely any timber. Then, on my right, I caught sight of the place I sought—a break in the ridge where it lifted in ledges clear to the top. I made for it.

Pop! Pop! Pop!

A few feet beyond the point where I must turn, somebody concealed in the brush was fanning a gun with the speed of an automatic. I felt a slug burn along my left thigh, on the outside, and another bit into my left arm. I leaped into the brush and tore my way toward the break in the hill, reached it and started up.

Pop! Pop! Pop!

The fellow in the brush was still fanning, and his lead was finding the rocks around my feet. That had to be stopped.

I leaped to cover behind a bowlder—and he made the mistake of opening up again. When he did I raked the spot he was in, locating it by the flare from his spouting gun, and when I ran from cover toward the top of the ridge, no more lead came my way.

I gained the top of the ridge, and plunged down its opposite side, thankful for the brush which clothed it. I had got away, carrying two wounds. That they were superficial I was certain, since I suffered no more than the sting and ache of them.

But, even so—where did that leave me? If Bill Leeds and his bunch were a part of Malvern's machine, then what? My wounds would mark me as the one who'd had the run-in with Leeds.

At that instant my eyes caught sight of a blaze of light far down on a wide ledge—and a man was crouching over it!

10

I TEAM UP WITH A BUZZARD

SQUATTING IN THE protection of a bush not more than fifty feet away from the camp fire on the ledge, and above it on a second ledge, I scanned the place closely. Only the one man was there, and he had a familiar look. Back toward me, he was in the act of cooking something on a stick over the blaze. After a couple of minutes he turned round to get a stick with which to poke his fire, and I recognized him.

It was the jungle buzzard—the bum Blinkey had struck across the face with the soup ladle!

What sort of reception would the buzzard accord me when I showed up at his camp? For that was just what I meant to do. Those wounds, slight though I believed them to be, needed attention. I didn't delay announcing myself.

"Hi, there!" I called, none too loudly.

The buzzard turned with a start, and his glance ranged the ledge above, while his right hand stole back to his hip.

"Never mind th' gun, bo!" I cautioned. "I'm not meanin' you any harm. Just want to talk to you a minute, and get you to do something for me. Shall I come down?"

"Come on," the man said. "But don't start nothin'!"

A moment later I was beside him. A great, red streak across the right side of his face testified to the efficacy of

Blinkey's ladle; it was a nasty scald, and must have been very painful. But there was a change in the appearance and manner of the jungle buzzard. Subtle, but unmistakable. I missed that hangdog air he had exhibited while in the jungles, and his eyes held level with mine when he looked me over.

"Well?" he asked gruffly.

"Guess you remember me?"

"Sure."

"I'm glad you do. Hear some shootin' awhile ago?"

"Thought I did. Couldn't be sure, though. Over the ridge from here, wasn't it?"

"Yeah. I got a couple of burns outa it, an' I need some attention. You've got water, I see, and my undershirt will make good bandages—"

"Any danger of anybody comin' over th' ridge after you?" he broke in.

"I know two that won't," I replied. "The others may. That's where you can help—if you've got guts."

His face reddened. "Listen, bo!" he almost snarled. "Somethin' happened to me last night that woke me up—understand? You saw it happen. I reckon th' manhood in me was just sleepin' a good, long sleep. But, by God, it wasn't dead! That lick across the face woke it—and I got guts enough for anything now!"

I nodded. So that was it! That was the change I had sensed in this jungle buzzard!

"Then you ought to thank your lucky star that Blinkey clouted you one," I told him. "Now, do this for me, and maybe there's a favor or two I can and will do for you. Climb up to the top of the ridge, where I came over—you can't miss the spot, because it's where the hillside breaks down into the cañon—and watch. If anybody shows up—say, you gotta gun? Wasn't stalling when you made that hip motion?"

"I got one—and a good one."

"Then, if anybody shows up before I'm through down here, let 'em have it. You'll be doin' a good job in bumping off any of them skunks—but I needn't tell you that. Will yu do it?"

He looked at me for a moment, then nodded. "I'll see you through," he agreed. "Since you've got wounds and need help, I'll give it. Get busy."

He started climbing toward the top of the ridge, and I proceeded to strip. Neither wound was in the least dangerous, but they felt better after I'd bathed and bandaged them. When I had finished I called to the buzzard, and he rejoined me.

"Not a sign of anybody," he reported. "Now, while I eat that rabbit I'd just cooked when you showed up, suppose you tell me what happened. Or maybe you don't want to?"

I told him about the fight that occurred after he was booted out of the jungles, and that the later fracas was an aftermath of that. It was easy to see that the chap had got a new grip on his nerve; that he was, in short, a greatly changed man. And a soup ladle had done it!

Self-respect—that is what he had regained. Sometimes, when it looks as though a man's pride is dead and the man himself begins to accept that viewpoint, a thing happens that revives it—and it turns out that it has only been lost for the time in a long snooze. So it appeared to have been in the buzzard's case.

While he devoured the rabbit, after I had declined to share it, I indulged in some quick thinking. After a bit I asked a question.

"I take it that you're aimin' to get Blinkey?"

He looked at me steadily, then said: "Well, what then?"

"Nothin', only I'm not sayin' nothin' against it," I replied. "He's got it comin' to him, an' no loss to th' world if he gets it—"

"*If* he gets it!" snapped the buzzard. "You mean *when* he gets it! Didn't I tell you that my self-respect has come back?"

I nodded. "I can see that it has, with half an eye. But, while you're resting up before tackling the job of getting Blinkey, maybe you'd take on something for me? Something that will put a hundred dollars in your pocket."

He looked straight into my eyes, then his wavered, dropped, came back. "I reckon not," he replied. "A week ago I might have put in with you, no matter what the graft happened to be. Now it's different."

"This thing I want you to do is something for society," I told him, leaving off the vernacular, "not against it. A chance, old man, to do something clear and decent. Any objection to lending yourself in that direction?"

He gave me a hard stare, then a look of comprehension crossed his face. "Humph! I've got your number, I think," he said. "Suppose you tell me what it is you want me to do."

"A simple thing. Make your way to Murphy's number one camp as quickly as you can, and deliver a message to Big Joe. I'm going to tell you just what you are to say, and then you can judge as to whether you will be the messenger.

"Go to Murphy in private. Tell him this: Tell him that

Jughead is crooked, and that Mike, the camp boss, is against him—with Malvern. Say that you got it straight from T.N., whom you met in the jungles, and that you are acting for him. Tell him T.N. said you were to be paid a hundred. Do you get that much?"

He nodded, and I went on.

"Tell him to expect big trouble to-morrow night—to-night, it will be then—and to gather all the men he knows he can rely on, arm them, and prepare for whatever may happen. I don't know just what is on the cards, but there's something—"

"You bet there's something—and it begins right now!"

I leaped to one side, and rolled away from the fire, almost at the moment the woods rang with revolver shots. Crashing through a low bush, I crouched low behind it.

The buzzard stood there with a smoking gun in hand, while on the ground lay the man who had burst so suddenly upon us.

It was Jughead Jones, Murphy's stable boss!

11

CAUGHT LYING

"**BACK FROM THAT** fire!" I yelled.

The Buzzard leaped—and just in time.

From the top of the ridge, whence I had descended when I came upon the tramp's fire, spurts of flame stabbed the night, and bullets rained down.

"Make for where I told you!" I shouted to the Buzzard. "Remember, it's a chance to get back at Blinkey!"

Swinging my gun toward the top of the ridge, I raked the rocks and brush with lead, hoping to halt the oncoming yeggs until my companion and I could drop away into the timber of the lower ledges. Near at hand, the Buzzard answered:

"I'm with you! Make your getaway! I know my way about!"

Then I heard him crashing away through the brush.

I struck off in another direction, reloading as I ran, with the jungle camp as my immediate objective. Long Bill Leeds had been the only man among those in the cañon who had recognized me. I felt sure of that, because the other had been too far away. Jughead Jones was dead. So was Bill Leeds. If I could get to Blinkey at once I might still be taken into his confidence and learn what was afoot for the following night.

Six-guns still roared and flashed above me, and the gang fairly fell down the ledges toward the embers of the Buzzard's fire. I was safely away, however, and had only to cover the ground between me and the jungles with all speed. That I endeavored to do. While running, I planned.

I won't soon forget that five-mile sprint. It was down one ridge and across a valley, then up another ridge and down again, and on and on over the roughest kind of going. I had the satisfaction of leaving my pursuers behind, though, and that counted for much.

Finally, just as I was on the verge of exhaustion, I sighted the jungle fire. A moment later I staggered into camp—and I wasn't stalling about staggering, either.

"Whut th' hell!"

The exclamation came from Blinkey who, with a dozen others, was sitting beside the fire. He leaped up, staring wide-eyed at me.

I dropped down on a chunk of wood, sputtering and gurgling. Blinkey's eyes were glued to my left shirt sleeve, and I realized that the exertion of my run had started the blood—that it had soaked through and dyed the sleeve.

"In—a minute!" I gasped. "I gotta—get my—wind!"

"I'll say yu needs it!" he exclaimed. "Whut yu run into?"

"I went—to Murphy's camp," I explained after a moment or two, "an' seen Jughead Jones. Guess whut else I got to say had ought to be said to you, by yoreself."

Blinkey walked away from the fire, motioning me to follow.

"Now—about Jughead?" His voice was sharp, and that

single glittering eye of his was disconcerting, considering what I was about to attempt.

"Jughead said for you to put me on," I told him. "Said you'd understand."

Silence. Then: "Who sent yu to Jughead?" he demanded.

"Nosey Conners."

He took a closer look. "Yu know Nosey pretty well?"

"I shore do."

"Wait a minute then. Nosey is right here in camp. I'll fetch him."

He strode away toward a near-by hut. Nosey was in camp! Should I run, or stand my ground? I resolved to stick it out. Run later—maybe.

Presently Blinkey and Nosey came over to me. "This gent says he knows yu well, Nosey," Blinkey said. "Says yu sent him to Jughead. Take a look at him, and say if he's tellin' it straight."

The broken-nosed skinner stared hard at me, then a look of recognition passed across his face. " 'Course, I knows him!" he exclaimed. "This here is Sandy. Me'n him knows each other well. Worked together. Think I'd send a man to Jughead without I knowed him?"

Was it the memory of those jolts of snow that turned the trick in my favor, or was the skinner afraid to admit that he had sent a stranger to the stable boss? I never learned the answer to that, but I got the benefit of his lie, whatever inspired it.

"Well," Blinkey said, his tense figure relaxing and his eye losing its threatening gleam, "that's diff'runt. Jughead told me to put you on—for what?"

But I had the answer. "For a little job that's to be pulled to-morrow night," I answered unhesitatingly.

"Yu can git back to bed, Nosey," Blinkey told the skinner. "I wanta talk to Sandy, an' by hisself." After we were alone: "Here's whut I wants to talk about. Whut did yu git into? Answer me that, an' then I'll put yu wise to whut yu are to do to get that five hundred."

"I'm shore aimin' tu tell you all about it. Afore I left Murphy's camp, Jughead—which same I happen to know, just like I does Nosey—told me to wait an' he'd string along with me. Said there was a meetin' goin' on back in th' jungles, an' he had to be there. He didn't say whut th' meetin' was about, ner where it was to be held. We ketched a lift on a freight wagon, stopped at th' steel-gang camp, then went on.

"When we gits to a place on th' dump about five miles frum here, we sees a man sneakin' along th' dump. Jughead tells me to wait, and pulls me down behind some rocks. The sneakin' gent comes on—an' it turns out to be that buzzard yu run outa camp last night. Him, an' nobody else. He tuck to th' timber, and Jughead 'lows we'd better follow an' see whut he's up to.

"Well, we ain't followed far until we hears guns a goin'. We runs on, an' th' shootin' gits worse. A mile back in th' woods, we stumbles over a man layin' in th' trail, an' he's dead. It's Big Bill Leeds. That ain't all. Th' buzzard is runnin' up th' ridge an' we are hot after him. Comin' to th' top, we loses him.

"We don't lose him fer long, though. He's hit, it seems, an' far down th' other side of th' ridge he builds hisself a little fire ah' starts tyin' up his wounds. Then we drops down onto him.

"But we are away off. He's not by hisself. Seems like this here fire has already been built, an' somebody's been waitin' there fer him. That somebody open up on us, an' I gits two holes in me.

"Jughead," I paused. "Jughead gits shot dead!"

Would that yarn go down? I wondered, almost holding my breath. Blinkey had satisfied himself that I was a skinner. Nosey, evidently in the ring with him, had vouched for me. I had my wounds to show for my part in the battle, and there was the buzzard, whom he might easily suspect. But—would he swallow the tale?

"Yu—yu ain't lyin'?" he almost gasped, boring into me with his glittering eye. "Jughead done got his? Shore enough?"

"I'm tellin' th' truth!" I declared. "Jughead Jones is dead!"

"God Almighty!" Blinkey almost whimpered. "An' he was one of my best men! Old Murphy never once suspected him! An' jest when we was about to finish th' play—"

"Shut yore mouth, yu damned fool!" a voice blazed almost at our side. "He's lyin', damn him! He's a cop! I didn't only git creased, an' I'm live as he is—a damn sight liver than he'll be in another minute!"

The speaker—blood-stained, and white with exhaustion—was Jughead Jones in person!

12

"WE'LL KILL YU IN PRIVATE!"

"STOP! NOT HERE, you fool!" It was Blinkey speaking. With a swift movement he thrust aside the gun Jughead had thrust against my chest and, at the same time, seized my right wrist in a powerful grip.

"Lemme git him now!" the stable boss begged. "Ain't he done kilt Long Bill an' Sam Brady? Ain't he a damned, sneakin' cop—"

"Shut up!" Blinkey snapped, stripping me of my gun. "Whut's th' diff'runce whether he's kilt here or somewheres else? He's shore goin' to git it anyhow! How does we know who may be here in th' camp?"

Then he turned to me.

"So yu put it over on me, an' a lot of us? Thought yu'd get by with yore smartness, didn't yu? Well, yu ain't goin' to! Yu are goin' to die, but we'll kill yu in private!"

"Reckon yu're right, Blinkey," Jughead conceded grudgingly. "May be some more damned cops among us here. Likely they is. Best to git rid of this'n where they ain't nobody to see. Whar at?"

Blinkey made no answer, but whistled shrilly. In a moment Nosey Conners came trotting up to us.

"Git a rope," Blinkey commanded, and Nosey went after it.

A few minutes later, with my arms roped to my sides and Jughead holding to one end of the rope, we set off into the timber back of the camp. Blinkey led and Nosey, who had made no comment so far, brought up the rear.

As for myself, I had not opened my lips in speech since Jughead appeared so suddenly and unexpectedly. It was a slip up, I grant, but it could not have been avoided. Those fellows blazing away at the Buzzard and me, after Jughead fell, prevented me from making sure that the stable boss was dead.

I thought it unlikely that the Buzzard could have failed to kill at so short a distance. However, he had shot without the time to take even the slightest aim. So, all in all, I exonerated him. The thing which disturbed me most, aside from the fact that I was being led away to die, was this:

I had no inkling of the nature of that final move Blinkey was about to make on the following night—the one in which I had been slated to take part. Had Jughead delayed his arrival a short while, I might have got the information from Blinkey, and made a sneak before he got there. For I had no intention to trust too much in the cock-and-bull yarn I had fed the jungle cook on. There were too many chances for a leak. It had been my intention to depart from the jungle camp at the earliest possible moment after I learned what I came for.

But—the cup had slipped.

Blinkey was speaking:

"Long Bill knowed what he was talkin' about," was his comment. "An' I'll admit yu shore did frame things fine.

How many days yu been hangin' aroun' these jungles, afore yu showed up last night?"

I made no answer.

"Damn yu!" he grated. "Yu aim to keep yore mouth shut, huh? Well, that won't git yu nothin', an' I know a way yu could be made to spill, if I had th' time fer it. But I ain't. Things is happenin' too fast aroun' here, an' I got other things to do. Wasn't fer that, bo, I'd love to make yu squirm awhile afore yu croaked—that fer bumpin' off two better men than yu are! Say, Jug," he demanded, "whut wus yu doin' there where yu got shot?"

"I was goin' to th' jungles to meet Long Bill an' th' others, when I heard a big ruckus. Guns a goin' to beat hell. I was makin' along th' top of th' ridge when I seen a fire. That's how come me to find that buzzard an' this here cop. That's how it happened. After they left, thinkin' I was dead, some of th' boys come down th' ridge an' told me about Long Bill an' Sam. We scattered, lookin' fer this gent here an' the Buzzard, an' I 'lowed he'd maybe make fer th' camp. That's how come me to show up."

"Uhuh. Lucky yu did. I was jest about to spill things, damn me! Seems like yu made a big mistake, Nosey, when yu said yu knowed this here bird. How come?"

The skinner made no answer for a moment, then muttered something so low I did not catch it.

"Hey? Speak up!" Blinkey ordered.

"He's a dead ringer fer th' one I thought he was—"

"Yu lie!" Blinkey broke in. "He's goin' to be a dead ringer, though. A dead ringer fer a stiff! Yu bungled, Conners—else yu're a sneakin' double crosser!"

"Honest to God, Blinkey!" Nosey Conners cried, his

voice pleading. "I ain't no double crosser! Take my word fer it! I thought I knowed him! Shore thought I did!"

Blinkey's answer was a snort of contempt.

"Blinkey," Nosey went on, "I ain't never been around where nobody was kilt like yu aims to kill this feller, an' I don't want to be! Lemme go back—"

"Yu goes right along with us—an' that ain't all yu does! Don't lemme hear another whimper outa yu!"

Silence then, while we stumbled along over the rocks and through the short undergrowth. Half an hour passed, and we came at length into a secluded hollow between great bowlders. There we stopped.

"This here is th' place I been headin' fer," Blinkey announced. "Right here, Mr. Kay-See Cop, yu gits croaked. Yore friend Nosey is goin' to do th' croakin'—"

"God!" Came in a bleat from the skinner. "I ain't! I can't—"

Blinkey, transformed into a living picture of Satan at his worst, wheeled, and I saw a knife flash in his hand. Nosey Conners had time for only a strangled cry of fright and agony, then he crashed backward into a clump of brush, struggled for a moment, then grew quiet.

13

A DYING BURDEN

"**TH' DAMNED YALLER** pup!" the camp cook snarled, wiping his wet knifeblade on some leaves. "He might of knowed I aimed to kill him, too! Anybody which double crosses Jeff Nolan is as good as dead! That's whut he done, an' I got him. That's whut Big Joe Murphy done, an' his time's a comin'! "That's whut yu done, damn yu!" he went on, his voice raised to a high pitch and his eye now resembling that of an enraged tiger. "Yu gained my confidence, then worked ag'in' me! Now yur time has come!"

At that moment I spoke, though I had no hope of stemming the tide of this demon's fury:

"Before you go any further with this slaughterhouse stuff," I said, "it may be as well for you to know a few things. In the first place, the man you thought was a jungle buzzard is anything but that. He's a mighty keen cop, and he's got you dead to rights. No matter what you pull here, you won't get away with it, for he knows who you are and what you are. Sooner or later, you'll pay. Now, go ahead, if you're so minded."

It was a lie, of course, but it might work.

"Hell! Do yu think Jeff Nolan cares how many cops has

been trailin' him here in th' jungles?" Blinkey demanded, his fury no whit abated. "Whut kin they do?

"I'm turnin' th' last trick to-night, instead of to-morrow night. I'm cagey, bo! An' I'll be where they ain't goin' to find me! Whut ever else Jeff Nolan may be, he ain't no fool! Big Joe thought he was, but he's found out diff'runt! "

"What did Big Joe ever do to you?" I asked, more to gain time than because I was really interested. Time, in my position was worth sparring for!

"None of your damned business!" Blinkey snapped. "Big Joe knows, an' Jimmie Doyle knew! Jimmie Doyle's dead, now—damn him! Tony Malvern knows, too, an' that's why he got me to—"

"Yu're goin' too far, Blinkey!" Jughead Jones interrupted. "Yu're mad, else yu'd have better sense! Even if this here cop is goin' to be dead in another minute or two, they ain't no use in yur doin' all that talkin'!"

Blinkey, though still shaking with rage, subsided. But he had given away a good deal. The knowledge might never do me any good, but I had learned what I had suspected all along: That there was something else back of all the destruction of life and property in Big Joe's camp. It had seemed queer to me that Tony Malvern would instigate and carry on such viciously criminal acts merely for sake of a fifty thousand-dollar bonus.

What had Big Joe Murphy done to incur the undying hatred of this demon, Blinkey? This devil of the jungles. This Satan, rampant in hell's back yard!

I asked myself the question, but could find no answer.

"I reckon I'll say th' rest of whut I have got on my mind," Blinkey said, in answer to Jughead's remonstrance, "to Big

Joe in person—jest afore I sinks my knife in him! As fer yu, yu damned sneak—"

"Put your hands high!"

The command snapped with deadly brittleness and, wheeling, I saw the white face of the jungle buzzard, the red mark of Blinkey's ladle across it. He stood not more than ten feet away, partly concealed by the brush, his six-gun trained on the cook.

Blinkey's action was swift and unexpected. With knife in hand, he lunged toward me, struck, missed by an inch, then leaped backward into the brush.

As I swung away from his knifestroke, I came abreast of Jughead Jones. Lowering my head, I butted him full in the stomach, saw him go down writhing, then plunged into the brush where the Buzzard was.

"Quick!" the latter exclaimed in a whisper. "Run for it! I haven't got a single load in this gun!"

We were both running, and as we ran I wriggled free from the rope. Through the undergrowth we crashed, for I had no wish to face the demon back of us with no weapon save an empty gun.

Fifty feet distant from the scene of my escape, I came to a dead stop. A groan, almost at my feet, had caught my ear.

"Don't leave—me!" came a plea. "That devil—Blinkey—"

I stooped over the chap who lay on the ground, and the next instant was running again—carrying a dying man on my shoulder.

The dying man was Nosey Conners.

14

INTO THE BEYOND

I KNEW IT would be only a matter of a few minutes before Blinkey and Jughead were hot after us, and the burden I carried lessened our chance of escape very materially. Why carry Conners, since he was in all probability at the very door of death?

Two reasons: One, the human reason, I will not dwell upon. The other was this:

Maybe Nosey would cling to life long enough to tell me a few things I desired very much to know. Just how much he knew of the plans of Blinkey and his gang was problematical. He might know all, or he might know but little. It was worth a chance.

I had my reward in another way, at any rate. I became conscious of something hard and heavy cutting into and numbing my shoulder. Lowering Nosey to the ground, I called to the Buzzard to wait. Another moment and I drew the skinner's six-gun from his belt—and it was loaded. In a pocket of his coat was a box of cartridges.

The dying man—he was dying, and going fast I could see—stirred, opened his eyes, then gasped:

"Am—am I—goin' to—kick off?"

"You are, Conners," I told him. "That was a deep wound

Blinkey gave you, and I think you can't last many minutes. Here," I said to the Buzzard, "try these cartridges in your gun. Both the same caliber."

"They fit," he assured me, a moment later. "Now maybe we'll make a stand. What do you say?"

"Listen for them," I instructed. "Conners," I went on, "you can't live—so why not come through?"

"Sure—I'm—a goner?" he said pleadingly, clutching my hand.

"As sure as that I'm here with you," I answered. "Tell me what I want to know, and I'll even things with Blinkey. First, what is the play they are to pull to-morrow night?"

Nosey closed his eyes, and his lips came together in a firm line.

"They're coming!" the Buzzard warned. "Running through the brush!"

"When they get closer," I replied, "let 'em have a few slugs. I want to hear Conners say something, and we're not going to run with guns in our hands."

"Right!" said the Buzzard, and took his station beyond me, behind a tree in the direction the cook and stable boss could be heard coming.

"Come, Nosey!" I insisted. "Help me get even with Blinkey—he stabbed you without cause! He's got it coming to him!"

Conners stirred—and at that instant the Buzzard's gun roared. There was an answering shot, and again the Buzzard's gun thundered.

"Quick!" I cried, shaking Conners. "Tell me!"

"They're goin' to blow—th' dam—at Sand Creek!" he

gasped weakly. "Let—water in—on—camp number—two—God! I'm a-goin'! Hold onto—me—Sandy—"

Bang! Bang!

The Buzzard was firing again, and the two men in the brush beyond were returning it. They had halted for the time at least, and the Buzzard appeared to be holding them.

"Get—Blinkey!" came from Nosey's white lips. "He's th'—main—one! Th' brains—of—it! Mike—Jughead! Malvern—pays! It's hell—to—go like—I'm goin'! It—shorely—is—hell—"

A convulsion—and he had passed out. The poor weakling—Nosey, the snowbird, was away on his last "sleigh ride" on the slopes of eternity.

Dragging his body to one side, I covered his face with a leafy brush torn from a small tree, then unlimbered my gun and got into action. At the same time I called to the Buzzard:

"This way! We haven't any time to lose!"

He joined me immediately, and we ran on for perhaps three hundred yards. Then I darted aside into the brush, and the Buzzard plunged in behind me. We crouched there, silent, watchful.

Blinkey and Jughead were no longer to be heard. They had lost our trail in the darkness.

"Conners—is he dead?" the Buzzard asked.

"Yes," I replied. "But before he went he came through with what I wanted most to know. There's work ahead—hot, deadly work. Do you want in on it?"

"Yes!"

That ladle was still working!

"All right. You'll not regret it. Now, how did you find me?"

"I saw, when it was too late, that Jones wasn't dead," was the answer. "I'd fired all my cartridges, and couldn't do anything about it. When he struck off toward the jungles in the direction you had taken, I followed. Was close when you were taken, and followed to where Conners was stabbed. Tried a bluff—and it worked. That's all."

"It's not all, by a damned sight!" I contradicted feelingly. "But we'll talk about that later. In the meantime, let's be moving—for, if I'm right, there's going to be a lot of powder burned before daylight! "

Wipe out Murphy's camp number two, would they? Well, maybe not!

15

AT CAMP NUMBER ONE

WE STRUCK OUT for the railroad dump, angling east and giving the jungle camp, where I was fairly certain Blinkey and Jughead had gone, a wide circle. It was my aim to get to Big Joe's camp number one as speedily as possible.

Bit by bit the plot, or double plot, against Murphy had been pieced together. The plot perhaps was one but there was a double motive behind it. Malvern's greed and Blinkey's hatred. I could understand the greed of Malvern, but could make nothing of the hatred of Blinkey.

Big Joe Murphy was never a man to oppress others. I had never known him to be intentionally unjust. Unless he had changed greatly since coming to Oklahoma, I felt sure that Blinkey's venomous activities against Joe had no root in any injustice of the latter's against him.

Yet the venom was there, as were the black deeds. Blinkey had hatred in his heart, and his brain and hands had been busily employed at its behest. Had Malvern chosen him to carry out his campaign of destruction, knowing his man and that he thirsted for revenge? Had he deliberately played upon those evil passions?

It looked like he had. Yet there was another angle worthy of consideration:

Had Malvern, after employing Blinkey, learned that he had bought more than he bargained for? Was it not possible that Blinkey had taken the bit in his teeth and run wild?

It seemed to me that some of the acts of the camp cook had been beyond the limit of what a sane man, such as Malvern must be in order to have achieved the material success which undoubtedly had been his, would sanction.

I could not vision him plotting the murder of Jimmie Doyle, for instance. Neither could I believe that the contractor would countenance so bold a thing as blowing up a dam and wiping out his competitor's camp and the work he had completed there. That didn't seem like the act of a sane man.

Granting that Malvern was of a stripe with his man Blinkey, would not his reason tell him that the blowing of the dam—an act which could have no other object than ruining Murphy—would be so suggestive of underhandedness as to point directly to him as the instigator? Malvern alone would gain by the dam's destruction.

On the whole, I began to believe that Malvern had, all unawares, unleashed a devil. But Malvern had unleashed him, and Malvern must therefore be adjudged equally guilty with him.

Those thoughts passed through my mind while the Buzzard and I made tracks toward the dump. We reached it, and paused for a consultation. The question was how to get to camp number one with the least possible delay. Ten miles to go, and nothing but our legs to carry us. Then the Buzzard remembered something.

"Got it!" he exclaimed. "The track-maintenance man keeps a speeder beside the dump a mile or so down the line. We can take that and make time until we reach the end of the rails. After that—"

"Come on!" I cried. "I've got an idea for 'after that!'"

We trotted down the track until we came to the speeder. It sat on a couple of short lengths of rail at the side of the track, and was locked. The lock defied us for about two minutes.

After that we were propelling ourselves along at a rate which threatened to land us in one of the numerous bar pits beside the way. We rattled through the steel-gang camp, and came to the end of the rails. There was yet four miles between us and camp number one.

"The stable tent of that gang that's rebuilding the blown up section of dump!" I said, pointing to where it stood half a mile from us.

We covered that half mile in a few minutes, and within a few minutes more were riding away on a pair of mules which we took from the tent—after an argument with the stable boss. It ended badly for him—got him a sore head at least—but there was no time to-waste. He'd be all right in an hour or two.

I'd lost the old silver turnip I had carried, and had no means of telling the time, but it was getting well along past midnight I felt sure. A lot of activity had been compressed within a few hours' time, and I felt my part in it in every bone and muscle. Still, the end was not yet.

We reached Big Joe's camp, and, doubtless because we were riding mules and not attempting to hide, reached his office without challenge. There we dismounted, and I pounded on the door of his shack.

Murphy, with Steel beside him, came to the door. Both had been asleep.

"Get your clothes on, both of you!" I bade them, pushing past them into the shack, the Buzzard following.

"Damned if it ain't Tug!" Murphy exclaimed, eyes wide. "But, lad, I hardly knew ye! What's happened to ye this night?"

"A lot," I answered. "This chap with me—I don't think I know what your name is?"

"Just call me Buzzard, and let it go at that," said the strange man with whom I had teamed up in so singular a manner.

"Suit yourself," I agreed. "Buzzard has done a man's work to-night, Joe. I'm telling you that now so you won't forget it. He's worth more than half a dozen ordinary men. I recommend him to you. And now where is the tent of your camp boss, Mike?"

"Mike? What's wanted of Mike?"

"Don't ask questions!" I snapped. "Lead me to his tent, and don't make any noise. You come along, Steel; there may be trouble."

Murphy, the Buzzard, Steel and I then stole quietly through the shadowy aisles between canvas walls until we came to a small tent off to itself.

"He's in there," Murphy whispered, pointing. "But, for th' life of me—"

With Steel at my heels I was inside the tent before Joe could finish his remark. Steel's flash light picked out Mike, who sat on his bunk staring in bewilderment toward the door, and we got him a split second before he got his gun.

Five minutes later he sat in a chair in Murphy's lighted quarters, a sullen look on his face.

I turned to Steel and the Buzzard.

"Introducing Mike, hireling of Malvern, and underling of Blinkey, the one-eyed cooker of jungle mulligan—and, incidentally, the most dangerous, cunning and vindictive cook who ever manned a ladle.

"Blinkey," I went on, turning back to Joe, "has another name. It is Jeff Nolan—do you know him?"

16

THE BUZZARD SPEAKS

"NOLAN!"

The ejaculation fell from Murphy's lips in tones of incredulity.

"Yes, Jeff Nolan. He's the chief tool Malvern chose to ruin you by. Our good Mike, here, and Jughead were bought by Blinkey with money furnished by Malvern. Doubtless Mike or Jughead blew up the powder shack, the dump, and burned the stable tent and the mules. I think they did those things together. I got it straight from Jughead that Mike is the one who killed Jimmie Doyle—"

I broke off in time to seize Big Joe, drag him from the cowering Mike, and hurl him into a corner.

"No violence, Joe!" I ordered. "Remember, you promised!"

"All right, Tug!" Big Joe grated, malevolent eyes upon the camp boss. "But th' damned snake is goin' to pay for that dirty deed! Mind you, he's goin' to pay!"

"Certainly," I agreed. "But the hangman will attend—"

"You cut that kind of talk!" yelled Mike. "Jughead Jones—where did you see him, and hear him say that?"

My lie about Jughead seemed about to produce results.

"I saw him in the timber near the camp where he was

to meet Long Bill Leeds, Sam Brady, and the rest of the gang. He didn't meet them, because Long Bill is dead, and so is Sam Brady. Nosey Conners is dead, too.

"Just before Jughead Jones left for the railroad station at Red Rock, with two of my men, he confessed to enough to hang every man we can catch—including Malvern. He swore that you stuck a knife in Jimmie Doyle's back—"

"Then he lied, damn him!" roared Mike. "Why in hell would he wanta saddle that on me? I didn't do it, and neither did he! Blinkey done it, and Jughead knows it!"

"Ah, so you accuse Blinkey? And why should he undertake that job, when he left all the others to his underlings?"

"Why? Just ask Joe Murphy if there'd be any reason why Jeff Nolan might wanta knife Jimmie Doyle!"

I swung round to Joe.

"Lissen, Tug," said the latter, "and I'll be afther makin' it all clear to ye. Whin I first come to Oklahoma and wint in business, th' firm name was Murphy & Nolan—Jeff Nolan holdin' but a small interest, and me th' rest. Jimmie Doyle, later, caught Jeff dead to rights when he was sellin' me out to me competitors. He tipped others off about me bids and got well paid for it. He stood to make more that way, he thought, than in takin' th' small legitimate profit from his share of work done.

"Well, th' proof was sthrong, and I kicked him out. Before he left he opened me safe, knowin' th' combination, and took five thousan' dollars of me money with him. But we caught th' dirty divil, an' he got five years.

"I remember, now, his term has been up for some time—but I niver thought he'd be afther comin' on to do me dirt, an' to kill Jimmie Doyle!"

"He probably was set on to do all the dirty work, by Tony Malvern—"

"No!"

The interruption came in ringing tones from the Buzzard. He stood erect before us, and there was nothing of the hang-dog about him then.

"Tony Malvern merely hired Nolan to harass Murphy as much as he could, delay the work, and all that," the Buzzard went on to explain. "But Blinkey went farther than that. Malvern tried to halt him, after the mules were burned, but he failed. What could Malvern do?

"If he took any drastic action against Blinkey, where would he be? You see, Malvern made the mistake of striking his bargain and paying over a big sum to Blinkey in the presence of witnesses—Bill Leeds and Nosey Conners. His hands were tied!"

"How do you know all this?" I demanded. "Who are you, anyway?"

For a moment the Buzzard hung his head, then he raised a flushed face to me.

"I must tell you, I suppose, in order to convince you that I know," he said. "My name is Henry Malvern—and I'm Tony Malvern's brother.

"But wait!" he exclaimed. "I want to say a few words more. Tony is lots older than I, and he brought me up in skinner camps—the only home he knows. I worked for him when I became old enough, on the grade at first to learn the business, then in the office. What could he have expected, living like that?

"I took to white-lime and coke, like I saw most of the hands doing, and he kicked me out. Since then, I've been wandering round, living in jungles, and trying to lose what little manhood that still clung to me. Nobody recognized me, because I have changed so in appearance.

"On the night Tony made his bargain with Blinkey, I was at my brother's camp. Had sneaked in there to beg money from him. Yes, I'd fallen that low. In an adjoining room, I heard all that was said between them.

"Let me add that I did not get the money, and that I have not seen Tony since.

"Something happened in the presence of this man here, whom I know only as Sandy, that caused a revolt inside me. I'm going straight from now on—and that's all I've got to say."

"And that's enough!" I declared, gripping the Buzzard's hand in mine. "You've proved yourself a man to-night, and I'm for you first, last, and always."

Then I said to the amazed Joe:

"I believe Malvern has told the exact truth, for I had already come to the same conclusion. Now," I went on, "if the gang should blow up a certain dam on Sand Creek, one near your camp number two, how near would that come to ruining you?"

Murphy's face grew white. "God, man!" he gasped. "That would ruin me altogether, it would!"

"Then," said I, "we'll be moving—for that's just what's on the cards for tonight—"

"No!" Mike broke in. "That job was planned for Wednesday night, and this is Tuesday!"

I glanced at Murphy's desk clock. "It is two o'clock Wednesday morning," I corrected. "It is true that Blinkey meant to blow the dam on Wednesday night, but when he lost three of his men and it seemed that the net was closing in, he decided to blow the dam at once.

"He boasted as much. Riding hard, and on horses instead of mules, he and his bunch could reach the dam in a few hours, and we've just about got time to prepare for the big blow-up."

Meaning a "blow-up" quite different from the one the jungle cook was aiming for.

17

THE DAM AT SAND CREEK

LEAVING MIKE UNDER guard of the commissary clerk and a timekeeper in whom Big Joe had confidence, we four, Joe, Steel, the Buzzard—for he'll always be such to me—and I, set out on a tour of the camp.

We separated and went with caution, it being our desire to make sure that all was quiet in and around number one. Finding all seemingly well, we gathered at the stable tent, saddled up and departed quietly eastward.

We knew that Blinkey and his gang could not yet have reached the dam, which lay four miles distant from the number one camp. Therefore, we could easily be on the scene to receive them.

But how receive them? Mike either did not know what part of the two-hundred foot dam was to be blown, or he pretended ignorance.

"All I know is that the dynamite is already planted," he insisted. "It's been planted for a week past. No, I can't say as any of th' guards on th' dam are in it. Maybe so, as it would have been a mighty hard job to get the stuff planted unless one or more of 'em was in th' know. I ain't saying as to that."

Beyond that he would make no statement. So we had two hundred feet of rock and earth embankment to choose from, any part of which might hold enough explosive to blow the whole thing to pieces.

We were not even sure that Blinkey would be there in person. It seemed likely, however, that he would not leave that to any one else, since most of his trusted men were absent. Too much depended on pulling the big coup. He would in all probability be on the dam, or very near to it.

That settled, I began trying to figure out the most likely point of attack on the dam. Not knowing the locality, I could make no headway there.

"Joe," I asked, riding abreast of him when we were nearing the site of camp number two, "have you any men here whom you can trust?"

"Tug," he answered sorrowfully, "I'm afther trustin' nobody! Look at Mike and Jughead! I'd 'a' swore by them lads—an' look at 'em! Th' dirty, treacherous, bla'-guards—"

"Forget 'em!" I admonished. "We four are a host. Blinkey can't have more than three or four men left at best. The rest must have been thinned out to-night. We'll handle the situation, but, I warn you—keep your wits about you, and keep close to me! Now, let's ride!"

We circled the camp and reached the sight of the dam a quarter of a mile beyond it. Sand Creek runs north and south at that point, and it was not that creek which had been blocked. West of Sand Creek a smaller stream angled across the valley and poured its waters into the larger. In order to avoid having to build a bridge across this creek, a dam had been erected which had turned the small creek into the larger at a point well off the right of way.

Needless to say, Joe had the dam under guard, since it was so important to him. The guards were our first lookout.

I climbed to the top of the dam and walked along it, Joe and the others following. Fifty paces farther along, Joe halted me.

"Hell!" he exclaimed. "There ought to 'av' been a guard at this end, but there's none here!"

"Come on!" I returned, and started running down the dam.

We reached the far end—and nowhere did we encounter a guard!

"They've gone!" Joe cried. "Sold out—"

"But how could they have known about Blinkey's change of plan?" I demanded.

"I don't know that! But they're not here, lad, an' no mistake!"

The Buzzard spoke:

"Might it not be that they were cautioned not to remain on the embankment at night, after the dynamite was planted?" he asked. "There was always a chance that a change of plan might be necessary—the date for the explosion set forward. For their own safety, might not—"

"You've hit it!" I applauded. "That's the explanation. Those guards—how many, Joe?"

"Two," he replied. "One at each end."

"Well, they're far from here at this moment," I told him. "And little blame to them, seeing they must know the character of the man they sold out to. Blinkey might have suddenly decided to blow the dam, and neglected to tell them about it. Granted, of course, that the fuse is planted where he can reach it unknown to them.

"Well, we at least know what end of the dam they will approach first," I went on. "It will be the end farthest from your camp, since they would come from the jungle camp on the south side of the stream."

I considered the situation for a moment, then gave orders.

"We'll scatter in the timber on this side of the creek, keep a sharp ear open for the sound of horses approaching. You three attend to that, and I'll see if I can unearth this dynamite plant of Blinkey's. Three revolver shots in rapid succession means get together. Get it?"

After they had gone into the timber to stand watch, I began scouting along the sloping side of the dam, using Steel's flash light to examine anything the nature of which the dim moon did not reveal to me.

On the upper, or land side, the embankment was almost perpendicular, supported by a massive wall of cemented rock; on the lower, or water side, it sloped gradually to the creek which washed it. On the latter side the footing was very insecure, and I had to make my way with extreme caution. Yet I felt certain that this sloping side would hold the plant. I thought so for two reasons:

That side would be hidden from the camp, and those who made the plant would have been better able to work unobserved. Secondly, it would be a comparatively easy matter to drill deep enough into the loose earth and rock which composed that side, than to do so in the rock wall of the upper side. Therefore, I searched the sloping side most diligently.

Suddenly, when no more than halfway along the dam, I saw a flare of light at the water's edge and about fifty feet beyond me—a match, I guessed instantly. The next instant I was in action.

Whipping out my gun, I fired at that little point of light—fired three times. I knew I'd found that plant at last, but had I found it in time?

The match went out, and the next instant a fusillade of shots rang out, the bullets singing about me. Down the dam raced Steel, the Buzzard, and Big Joe.

"What's up?" cried Steel, dropping down beside me.

"They've stolen a march on us! They came down Sand Creek in a boat—and the question is, did the match I saw get in its work? If it did, then this dam is going skyward in a mighty short time!"

18

BLINKEY'S KNIFE DRINKS BLOOD

AT THAT INSTANT a second match flared at the water's edge, and we were on our feet as one man, running down the dam toward it, shooting as we ran. That first match had failed!

We got bullets in return, too, but reached a point above the spot where the light had showed, without harm. There we flattened out and our lead fairly rained downward.

Bullets also clipped the earth and rocks about our positions, but we made poor targets at best. The moon was back of us, and the slope of the dam lay in deep gloom. We could only shoot into the darkness, hoping thereby to frustrate any further attempt to light the fuse which would, if ignited, result in exploding the dynamite which was cached beneath us.

Now and then a yell came up to us, and we knew that we had drawn blood. Yet they stuck on. Their gun-fire showed that.

Big Joe lay beside me, and his gun sent forth a steady stream of smoke, ceasing only for the few seconds required for reloading.

Then the gang below drew blood. It was Steel who suffered. He got a slug along the side of his neck when he leaned a bit too far over the edge, and the moon betrayed him.

Big Joe was next to draw lead—and it resulted in what appeared at the moment to be a disaster. His position was a precarious one, requiring considerable effort to remain balanced. When the bullet struck, he lost his balance, poised on the edge for an instant, then, before I could reach him with a free hand, slid over and plunged down the slope.

There was a loud splash when he hit the water, followed by a yell of glee from the crowd below.

Then, without the loss of a second, I was sliding downward on his heels. I do not know to this day who struck the water first, Steel, the Buzzard, or myself. I only know that we were all struggling there—and I thank the gods that be for waterproof ammunition!

There were two boat-loads of them. Evidently Blinkey had feared interruption, and that explained to me why he had wanted so many men along. He wanted them in case of a fight—and he was getting that fight!

In the first and nearest boat I could see a struggle going on, and I discharged my gun toward the second boat in order to do as much damage as I could in case it was fated that I, Tug Norton, was to pass out that night.

"Quick!" came in strangled tones from one of those who struggled. "Help, Tug! Help!"

It was Big Joe Murphy who called—and I saw red!

"Yu're too late, Mr. Cop!" Blinkey shrieked. "I told yu I'd sink my knife in him—an' here goes!"

I saw the gleam of steel in the dim light—then a figure shot past me, grasped the gunwale of the boat, capsized it, and the water was alive with struggling forms. I heard a shrill, blood-curdling yell, and the next instant the second boat bore down on me.

I got my third wound of the night, this one in the left shoulder, but it did not then hamper me seriously. I had found shallower water, and, standing up, I raked that craft, fore and aft, with lead.

Amid the din of shrieks and wails, I heard Big Joe shouting.

"All safe, Tug! Where are ye, lad!"

"Here!" I shouted.

He struggled through the creek to my side—and suddenly there was a deep silence over the water!

"How did you manage it, Joe?" I panted.

"I didn't!" he cried. "It was young Malvern! He turned the boat over just in time!"

"That shriek—who was it?"

"Blinkey!" he said. "That was when Malvern stabbed him to the heart with his own knife!"

Just then Steel and Malvern reported.

"If there's any more left, we can't find 'em!" Steel said grimly. "Maybe one or two escaped—but—I guess the water got 'em!"

But I was thinking of Blinkey and his knife. It had drunk blood again that night, just as he had said it would—but the blood was Blinkey's own!

19

THE MAGIC LADLE

BIG JOE MURPHY won the bonus. The fifty thousand dollars just about let him break even on his losses due to Malvern and the jungle cook. But that made little difference to Joe. He had made a fortune long ago, and continues in the game merely for love of it—particularly the fights it continually affords him. Joe is a fighter—but it is unnecessary to put that down here, since I have already said he is an Irisher.

He likes the atmosphere of hell's backyard.

I had his flourishing autograph awhile back, but did not keep it long. I scanned it closely in order to be sure it was genuine, then passed it through a wicket to the teller at my bank. It was worth five thousand more to me in the teller's hands, than if I had kept it handy merely as a memento.

Mike, the only member of the gang left alive, so far as we could determine, went to trial, but Big Joe failed to appear against him. So Mike went free.

Joe's reason for failing to appear against his former camp boss may be seen, should any one choose to visit him in Dr. Waldron's private sanatorium for the insane, at Kansas City. A mild patient, but mentally incompetent, notwithstanding.

Tony Malvern, when the full horror of the thing he had set going was made known to him, became a broken, doddering old man. Finally it was advisable to keep him under strict observation. Joe, on young Malvern's account, kept the matter under cover as much as possible. Mike's prosecution would have brought all to light.

But his situation might easily have been worse. As it is, he is tenderly cared for by his brother, Henry Malvern, erstwhile jungle buzzard, whom Blinkey's soup ladle so miraculously restored, and who took up Tony's business when he laid it down.

And so it may be seen that however loath I am at all times to indulge in gun-throwing, it is sometimes necessary to do it. When such is demanded, I earnestly endeavor to deliver.

THE SILENT PARTNER

*Where the Ozarks Rear Their Shaggy,
Weatherbeaten Heads—There a Memorable
Night Was to Be Made Hideous With Slaughter*

1

IN A STARTLING MANNER

MOST PEOPLE WHO have business with the Kaw Valley Detective Bureau, announce themselves at the door and are shown in by a boy kept for that purpose. That method of calling at an office is, I believe, considered usual the world over.

Upon occasion, callers brazenly crash the door and walk in. That method is considered rude the world over and it is the same with us.

One caller, however, entered my office in neither of those ways. He came in a manner most unusual—startling would be a better word.

I had been waiting after hours for him, in compliance with a request expressed in a letter. My afternoon mail had that day contained a communication which gave me a good deal to think about during ensuing spare moments.

Paper and envelope were such as are kept on sale in stores everywhere, and there was nothing to indicate the town where the letter was written. Just the date line, in pencil, and none too legible at that, and my name—Tug Norton—instead of the name of the bureau. Then the body.

At first it impressed me as being a simple request to grant the writer, Benjamin Lomax, an interview at ten

o'clock that night, stating that the writer would reach the
city late and could not present himself before that hour.
Nothing out of the way about that, except it kept me on
the job long after everybody else had called it a day.

It was the postscript which first got me to thinking
about the letter. As though it had occurred to the writer
that I might not remain so late for him, he added that large
interests were involved, and they were able and willing to
pay most liberally for the services required. That caught
me, of course. The combination of large interests and high
pay gets Tug Norton's attention every time.

Then I got to reflecting that these same "large interests"
used mighty poor stationery, Also that it was mighty secre-
tive stationery, since there was no printed heading, and, to
emphasize the element of secrecy, the town where written
was not given.

Of course there is usually the give away of the postmark.
But the postmark on this letter did not enlighten me; on
the contrary, it served to cloud the matter. The writer had
stated that he would reach Kansas City only in time to call
at my business office at ten o'clock the following night.

How, then, came it that the letter had been mailed in

He was staggering to and fro like a drunken man—
when I turned my eyes to the trail again.

Kansas City at nine o'clock on the morning of the day I received it? For the postmark showed clearly that it had.

I studied that last phrase over, and came to a conclusion which satisfied me: Mr. Lomax had intended mailing the letter from out of town, but later concluded to ask a few questions about my bureau before offering it his case; he had known that a letter, if mailed early in the morning, would reach me in time. He had advanced the hour of his departure accordingly. Had, in fine, arrived in Kansas City several hours before dropping the letter in the box.

Another explanation, one I hardly considered, was that he had been prevented from mailing the thing where he had intended to.

A lot of time wasted in speculation, you may say, since I had only to await the coming of Mr. Lomax and be enlightened. Perhaps so, but speculating about things, reading signs, making deductions, all are in my line. The letter interested me, and claimed my attention.

While I was eating supper that evening, another deduction hit me squarely between the eyes. It clinched the thought in my mind that Mr. Lomax desired secrecy—and lots of it. He was, clearly, afraid to be seen at or even near my office, else why had he made the appointment for ten o'clock?

It might be said that he had intended coming to Kansas City later. Perhaps so—but he had, in fact, arrived very early in the morning. Why could not he have made his call in daylight then? What could it mean?

Secrecy? Why the whole circumstance smelled of it a mile off!

Ten o'clock came, and with it the sound of footsteps in the corridor leading to my suite, which is on the second floor of the Sandstone Building, in the hotel district. I had left the corridor lighted, and the ground glass of my door would enable the caller to find my quarters easily, since it, too, was lighted. So I waited.

My client came on, a heavy man, judging by his tread, and his shadow suddenly loomed in front of the glass of the door. His hand lifted in the act of knocking—then the shadow disappeared, there was a short, sharp cry, and then a thud upon the floor.

My cigar fell from my fingers. I leaped to the door and flung it open. Then I sprang back as quickly, for the body of a man sprawled head first halfway across the sill. A blue spot in the center of his forehead, oozing blood, told a ghastly story.

The client for whom I had waited was dead.

2

WHENCE CAME THE BULLET?

NO SOUND HAD come to my ears save the low cry and the fall of the victim.

I touched a button which threw the corridor into darkness, drew my gun and stepped outside. A search of the place revealed no one, and it was clear that the killer had escaped. That would be easy enough, since he had only to make his way down the stairs and onto the street. There were two exits available, front and rear. He might be lurking in the building, but to search the entire place was out of the question.

I returned to the office, got Jim Steel, my chief assistant, on the phone, then examined the corpse. The next instant I was in the corridor again, surveying it in a new light.

Lomax had been shot in the forehead while he was facing a window at the end of the hall, and no assassin could have been hidden there, for the simple reason there was no place in which to hide. Mine was the last door at that end, and had a man been waiting there he would have been seen by Lomax immediately he turned the corner of the transverse hallway. Furthermore, he could not have passed my door after the shooting without casting a shadow on the glass.

No such shadow had been thrown upon it. Of that I was absolutely positive.

Almost above the spot where Lomax had been, a single bulb lighted the hallway, and a man standing before the door would have been strongly in relief. The position of the killer, at the time he fired, was no longer a secret.

He had been across the street in a room of the Mercedes Hotel.

I went to the window at the end of the hall and scanned the hotel building closely. I was on the second floor, and it was a reasonable conclusion that the killer had occupied a room on a corresponding floor of the hotel, since the third would have afforded little chance for such an accurate shot.

"He must have been in the room directly across from here, or in one of those flanking it," was my conclusion. "The one directly across would have given him a cinch shot, but it could have been done from the windows of either of the others. Gone now, of course."

I turned at the sound of footsteps behind, and discovered Steel coming almost at a run. Together we entered the office and further examined the corpse.

Secrecy again. Not one thing on the body to reveal its identity. A middle-aged man, gray-headed, and wearing a closely cropped mustache of the same color, he was dressed in a dark business suit, and wore stout, black walking shoes. A billfold gave up a considerable sum of money, and there was nothing else in the pockets except a knife, bunch of keys, and other articles commonly carried by men. One thing, however, gave me food for thought.

Each hip was armed with a formidable six-shooter of approved make and late model. They were new in another sense, too, since they had not been fired more than a few times each. Patently, Benjamin Lomax had been prepared for trouble.

"Call headquarters, Steel," I instructed, and departed for the Mercedes.

"Who occupies the three rooms on the second floor directly across from my office corridor, Don?" I asked the clerk. He considered for a moment, got the locations fixed in mind, then consulted his room list.

"They would be Nos. 222, 224, and 226," he informed me. "All vacant tonight."

"I want to look 'em over, and quick," I told him. "Send Bud Sampson, your house detective, up soon as you can locate him. Give me the keys."

I mounted to the second floor, keys in hand, and found Bud Sampson on my heels. "What the devil's wrong, Tug?" he queried.

"Man killed in the corridor outside my office," I told him, opening the door of No. 224. "Must have been shot from one of these three rooms. Only place from which it could have been done."

Room 224 showed no signs of having been entered since it was cleaned and locked by the maid that morning. No weapon of any kind, and not the slightest scent of powder smoke. Moreover, there were no holes in the window screens, and the dirt and trash in the crevices where they were set into the sash proved conclusively that they had not been recently removed.

"We draw a blank here," Bud said sarcastically. "The other rooms will be the same," he predicted. "What you trying to do, Tug, get us in the limelight?"

I made no answer, but when later I discovered that Nos. 222 and 226 betrayed the same conditions, both as to window screens and lack of evidence of recent occupancy, I was bound to admit that Bud had been partly right in the matter.

"We'll search the rooms above," I told him. "Hate to arouse your patrons, if the rooms are occupied, but it's important. Come on."

He went with me reluctantly. A thorough search of the three rooms on the third floor was barren of results. It would have been very difficult for a man to have fired accurately from the windows, and, to clinch matters, the screens were intact, and had not recently been removed.

"Admit you've been wrong, now, eh?" Sampson grinned, when we had made our search. "Must have been done by somebody in your own building. That's clear."

The squad from headquarters arrived then, made the same examination and came to a like conclusion.

"You are wrong, Norton," Sergeant Callaway declared. "Shot by somebody in the corridor with him. There's no question about that."

"But the killer could not have got by my door, after doing it," I argued.

Callaway grinned. "He could have been lurking in a cross corridor behind his victim, attracted his attention just as he was in the act of firing, and sent a bullet into his forehead when he turned. Could have happened that way, my boy."

But it hadn't happened that way. I had a clear view of the profile of Lomax when he went down, and he had been facing the window in the end of the corridor at the instant the bullet struck. I could not be mistaken. I didn't argue the point with Callaway, though. It would have been useless.

"You see, Tug," the sergeant pointed out, "all fire escapes in the Mercedes are of the late type—built inside fireproof walls. The window ledges could not have been reached from any possible position, and there is no other way a man could have maintained himself outside these rooms. You are on the wrong scent. Forget it. Headquarters will hand you the answer in the morning."

I gave him all the information I could. "Lomax, whom I don't know, wrote for an appointment, the letter being mailed here in the city," I said. "That's all I know."

"Humph!" Callaway commented. "Gang trouble, most likely. This Lomax is mixed up in something with others, wants out, goes to you for the purpose of spilling things, being afraid of the regulars, and gets bumped off. That's the answer, and we'll prove it."

"Step on it!" I snapped. "Do that, and you'll save me a lot of bother. But—you're going to get another slant at this case before many hours pass, sarge," I predicted. "When you are ready to confess failure, just call on me and I'll give you the facts."

"You go to hell!" rasped Callaway, and, followed by his squad, he departed.

I waited until sure they were out of the building and across the street, then I made for an exit as fast as I could go. I had been standing beside a window in room 224, and something in the street had caught my eye—something I desired to investigate without the loss of a minute.

3

IN A MELTING POT

I CROSSED THE street to a point on the sidewalk beneath the window through which I was certain the fatal bullet had been fired, and looked up. Nothing there but the cables of the telephone company, and they at a level with the top sill of the window.

One of those cables, however, showed a large, long lump—a joint which had been only partly spliced. Forty feet distant, close against a telephone pole, was a cable-splicer's canvas-inclosed platform.

The platform was in a position directly down the street from my office windows, and no human being could have fired a shot from it into the corridor window. But a cable-splicer's platform is movable. It swings from the cable on trolley runners—pulleys—and can be moved along in the air to any desired point between two poles.

The splicer's work for the day over, he draws the platform back to the pole by which he desires to descend, using a rope attached to the pole, the loose end fastened to the platform. It is a simple operation, seen every day in the streets. That, perhaps, is why it had appealed to the killer.

By means of the iron spikes driven into the telephone pole, I mounted to the platform, pushed aside the loose flap of the covering and got in. My flash light revealed nothing save the melting pot and tools of the operator—at first glimpse.

Resolving to test out my theory, I unfastened the rope and allowed the platform to drop easily along the sagging cable. With no difficulty whatever, I reached a point from which I could look into my corridor window.

The killer had been on that platform, just outside, when he fired the shot.

Convinced in my own mind, I then desired to establish beyond doubt that the platform had been so used. I went over the interior of that swinging canvas hut minutely—and found what I looked for.

It was inside the melting pot, buried beneath a mass of broken lead which the operator had gathered up from the floor and placed there on top of the hot lead at quitting time. In that way the waste lead is remelted and fused with the mass, after the fire is again glowing hot in the morning.

A silencer. No mistaking it, even though the killer had smashed it out of shape with a hammer before concealing it. Next morning that silencer would have been melted in the pot, and even though the splicer should discover some foreign substance in his lead, no one could have told what that substance was.

But it had not been melted. I put it into my pocket, and descended—and, in doing so, demonstrated another theory:

Not a soul on the street had challenged me as I moved along the cable in that hut. So accustomed are people in a city to seeing all sorts of tasks of that kind done at night, no one had seen anything out of the ordinary in a presumed cable-splicer doing an emergency job that hour.

The killer had figured that, too—showing that he had a good head, as well as good aim with a gun.

I started back to the office, resolving to say nothing at present about my discovery. Let Callaway boast. I'd perform. At the door I ran into Jim Steel.

"Hurry up, Tug!" he exclaimed. "Man on the wire who won't talk to anybody but you. Says he wants to ask about some business you will understand. The Lomax matter."

"What phone is he on?" I demanded, making a dash for the stairs.

"The one in your private office," Jim answered. "The cops in the outer office don't know anything about it."

"Good!"

I entered through a private door, and did not disturb the coroner and those in the main room.

"This is Tug Norton," I announced into the transmitter.

There was silence for a moment, then a man's voice came hesitantly:

"I'll have to take your word for it, I guess. At least, you're not the man I was talking to a few minutes ago."

"I'm Norton, right enough," I assured him. "What do you want with me?"

"Did you have a caller at ten?" came the query.

"Yes."

"That's been over an hour ago," the voice went on, "and he agreed to call me up from your office within a few minutes after he got there. What's wrong? Why didn't he call?"

"Maybe you'd better tell who you are," I suggested.

"Then, if I think you're entitled to it, I'll give you the information you ask."

"You ought to know who I am," came in surprised tones.

"I don't, though!" I exclaimed, allowing some heat to show in my voice. "And if you don't quit beating about the bush, I'm going to hang up right now! My time is valuable, and I'm not wasting it to-night. Get that?"

"No! Don't do that! I'm Ben Lomax, the man who wrote for an interview with you—"

"Then," I interrupted, "who is the man who really came?" I demanded.

"Dave Markey. I'm waiting at the Grand Hotel for him to report. Where is he—"

The voice broke off. There was a muffled exclamation, followed by a choking cry—then silence!

4

THE MAN IN THE RED MASK

CALLING TO STEEL to wait and answer questions, should the coroner ask any, I departed on the run for the Grand Hotel, four blocks distant. I wasted no energy speculating on what I would find when I reached the room from which the telephone call had come. I rather thought I'd find another corpse.

"Got a man by the name of Lomax?" I asked the clerk, pausing almost out of breath before the desk.

"Yeah. Room 482—"

I was on my way. When I rapped at the door of 482, I was astonished at getting an immediate answer.

"Who is it?" came the voice of a man, while the door remained closed.

"I'm Norton," I replied. "Open up, or I'll break in!"

"Thank God!"

The door opened, and the man who had uttered the pious ejaculation stood, white and trembling, before me. He was very much like the dead man in my office, in a general way, though nobody would have mistaken one for the other. The same age, and dressed pretty much alike. I could see him only by means of a dim light in the corridor, for the interior of the room was dark.

"Come in," he bade me. "I was never as glad to see anybody in my life," was his fervent pronouncement, after I had proved my identity. "Was sure you'd come—"

"Certainly," I interrupted. "But why the gloom? Can't we have some light on the subject?"

He stepped to a wall switch beside the telephone, and closed it. I noted that the curtains were drawn over the windows, and that the man cast frequent nervous glances toward them. I took a seat.

"Now, Mr. Lomax," I requested. "Tell me what happened when you were phoning. I rather expected to find a dead man here, but you seem alive enough."

Lomax sank into a chair, and the lines in his rugged, weather-beaten face deepened. "I'm alive, Mr. Norton, because the light switch happened to be near the telephone—near enough for me to reach. Otherwise, I should have been dead on this floor."

"Tell me about it."

"I had just begun talking to you, when a noise outside my window attracted me. I turned, and there, half across the sill, a pistol gripped in one hand, was a man whose face was completely covered by a mask—*a red mask.*"

He paused, shivered, and looked at me with eyes that reminded me of those of a condemned man with whom I once talked just before the dead march began.

I nodded. "A red mask. You have seen men in red masks before? Am I right?"

He gulped. "I have—several times. I'll add that not all who see that red mask live to tell about it. But I'll get on with the story.

"I cried out, at sight of the man on the sill, then I acted.

The light switch was within reach of my hand, and I threw the room into darkness, leaped away from the position I was in at the time, drew my own gun and waited. The intruder slowly withdrew from the room and closed the window. Not a word was spoken by either of us.

"After a time I went to the window, shielded by the darkness, and found that the fire escape outside was deserted. I then drew the curtains, and called your office. Presently you arrived, having already been on the way. That is all."

I shook my head negatively. "Not near all," I contradicted. "What, for instance, do you know about men in red masks?"

He looked at me blankly. "Why, Dave Markey surely has already told you the whole thing?"

"No, Mr. Lomax. Dave Markey was shot and killed in the corridor outside my door, before he entered the office. He did not have a chance to tell me anything."

Lomax got to his feet slowly, eyes wide and staring, face a chalk white. "Dead? Dave—Dave Markey—dead?"

"Yes. Just as I told you."

He shivered, sank back in his chair, covered his face with his hands and groaned—just once. A long-drawn groan of deep agony. After a moment he looked up, his face grim.

"Dave went to you in my place," he said. "I was being watched, and he insisted that he would be safe. I let him go! Good God! He died in my stead!"

I felt the grief of the man before me, but I also realized that valuable time was being consumed in doing nothing.

"You want to trap Dave Markey's murderer, it goes without saying," I remarked. "Now let's get to the gist of this business, and thereby expedite his capture. No use looking for the man who was on your fire escape. He's under cover long before this. Let me have your yarn. What was it that brought you to Kansas City after a detective? Also, and answer this first, why did not you notify the hotel office, as soon as the man in the mask disappeared?"

"That's the trouble, Mr. Norton," he explained. "In this matter the greatest secrecy must be used. I dare not make a move until I am sure of the protection I came to you hoping to get."

"A very good reason," I agreed. "Now, what is the nature of your danger, and how do you expect me to protect you?"

"I know the danger, right enough," said Lomax. "But you must answer the other question—if you can. I had hope when I came, but now I'm afraid the hope was ill founded. Mr. Norton," he went on, bending over and speaking in low tones, "the man who calls himself 'The Silent Partner,' and whose power seems unbreakable, is, I have almost come to believe, possessed of super-human means of divining every move against him—even before those moves are more than half formed thoughts!

"He is a devil! A fiend to whom human life is nothing; human woe his meat and drink!

"But you shall judge for yourself!"

5

"TO DISOBEY MEANS DEATH!"

AFTER A MOMENT of intense concentration, Lomax began to speak.

"You have been in the Black River section of Arkansas, Mr. Norton, and because of your activities there I was led to consult you about my case. I am from a different part of the river country—a wilder, more lawless section than you were engaged in.

"You may doubt that, since the river below Powhattan passes through some mighty rugged country, there is one inhabited by people to whom law is as nothing. But when you have visited that part of the river country which lies above Black Rock a matter of twenty miles, you will agree that all I say of it is true.

"Frankly, and to be brief, hell could be no worse.

"But it has not always been so. Illiterate, rough, lawless it has always been, but it was not until the coming of the men in the red masks, governed by one who has no other known designation than that of the Silent Partner, that the country lost all semblance of a civilized community.

"In Mussel Bend, a crescent shaped sweep of the Black, about twenty miles long, is located a number of pearling camps, each large, and each operated by a master pearler.

That is to say, a man who finances the work of taking pearls from the river, owning his camp and boarding his men. I am a master pearler—what is called, in our district, a big operator.

"There are fifteen so-called big operators working camps in Mussel Bend. Each is independent of the other. We sell, for the most part, to traveling buyers who make the district regularly. Six months ago there were eight or ten such buyers; now they have been thinned down to five. You'll understand why they have been thinned out, a bit later on.

"Up to a year ago, Mussel Bend was no better and no worse than other pearling camps along the Black—which is bad enough. We were, however, comparatively quiet. Then trouble began.

"Oscar Knowlton, a prosperous operator, was driving a buggy over a road back in the hills above the bend, when he looked up to see a man standing in the middle of the road. A man dressed in a suit of dark clothing, black slouch hat and riding boots. But the startling thing about his costume was this:

"His face was completely covered by a red mask.

" 'Reach for a gun, and you die where you sit!' came the admonition. 'I have no intention of harming you, unless I am forced to do so. Neither do I want your money, watch, chain, or other valuables. I merely want to introduce myself. I am your silent partner.'

"Knowlton, astonished at first, then became convinced that some one was playing a joke. He ordered the jokester out of the road, and was about to drive on.

" 'Stop!' came a command so menacing that Knowlton jerked his horse to a sudden halt. 'You are flirting with

death!' the man in the red mask went on, his tones cold
and deadly. 'I am, as I have already said, your silent partner.
By no means am I a robber, and must not be so considered.
Listen—and let this sink in!

" 'Being your silent partner, I desire a share of your profits. Not only desire a share, but intend to have it. It is now
the first day of the month. On the tenth you will travel
alone to the top of Dead Man's Bald, which lies two miles
to the west, and place the sum of ten thousand dollars in
currency on top of Nathan's Rock—you know the place.
You will then return to the valley. When I desire a second
division of our profits, I shall advise you. Do you understand?'

"The thing was so incredible, so ridiculous, Knowlton
burst into a hearty laugh. Surely this was a fine joke!

"But it was no joke. Knowlton's right hand held the
reins, and before the echoes of his laughter had died away,
there was a sharp report from the gun of the man in the
road—and the little finger of Knowlton's right hand was
shot clean off!

" 'Still think I'm joking?' the man in the mask demanded.
'That ought to convince you differently. What I've just
done is nothing to what will happen if you fail to carry
out my instructions to the letter. Fail, or try any tricks such
as putting the money on the rock and then trying to trap
me, and your camp will be raided and you will be killed.
Remember, I do not express my wishes but once—and to
disobey means death!'

"He vanished in the brush beside the road. Knowlton
drove at a gallop back to camp and had his wound dressed.
For a few days he kept his own counsel, then informed a

few of his closest friends among the operators of what had
occurred.

"Imagine their indignation! One and all advised Knowlton to sit tight; to disregard the wishes of his silent partner.
Why, the thing was not to be thought of! The monumental
impudence of the demand!

"Mr. Norton, Knowlton listened to the advice of his
friends—and on the night of the eleventh of the month
his camp was sacked by a band of men—variously esti-
mated at from ten to twice that number, and all wearing
red masks—and Knowlton was shot dead!"

Of course, I had seen that denouement coming all along,
else Lomax would not then have been relating the story to
me. Nevertheless, I was a bit startled when it came. I waited
for him to proceed.

"The next operator to meet his silent partner," Lomax
resumed, "was my brother-in-law, Peter Brady. He met
him on a road close to the river, one used in reaching the
ferry three miles above Mussel Bend. Virtually the same
instructions were given by the man in the mask—with
this difference: 'Remember Knowlton!' he cried, just as he
disappeared in the brush.

"Now Peter Brady was a brave man. He resolved to trap
the Silent Partner, as he was soon to become known all
over the district. To make it short, Peter took the money—
ten thousand dollars—up on Dead Man's Bald, and left
it on Nathan's Rock. Then he went away. In the brush of
the hilltop many armed men were hidden. But the money
remained there on the rock. No one came for it—and that
same night, Peter's camp was sacked, and he was killed!

"For a time thereafter, the highwayman did not trouble

the operators in the Bend. But he was not idle. He merely transferred his attention to the traveling pearl buyers. They, having the terrible example of his operations among the master pearlers before them, paid up on demand. In no case did the bandit rob a pearl buyer of all he carried, but insisted upon an equal division.

" 'I am not a bandit,' he would say. 'I'm a partner in your business—a silent partner.'

"Imagine the impudence of it! As a result, most of the buyers have quit that section of the river. Then the thief got busy among the operators again.

"Of course, the whole district is aroused, and State and county officers are very active thereabouts. Operators are careful not to travel the roads alone, and always take armed guards with them. Those precautions make no difference. The operators began receiving written 'duns,' as the writer called them.

"Most operators who receive such demands, found unaccountably in their tents, or, in one or two cases, received through the mail, obey them. One, Ralph Peck, failed to do so, and established a heavy guard around his camp at night. Nothing happened for two weeks. The guards were withdrawn—and on the very night of their withdrawal Peck's camp was raided, and he was killed.

"No amount of searching has revealed the least trace of the hangout used by the bandit and his men. That, however, is not to be wondered at, since the hills back of the river are so wild and rugged as to be almost impenetrable. Also, the very men who constitute his band may be working among us during the day. The faces of none of them have ever been seen.

"My dun came in the course of time, and I paid. Markey paid. Then, upon being summoned a second time to produce, I resolved to do all in my power to rid the district of the Silent Partner. He is sucking it dry, just like it was a huge orange.

"To that end, a letter was sent to you, asking an appointment. Dave and I took every possible precaution to prevent our real destination from becoming known. He went east to Memphis, ostensibly to consult a physician about an operation which he let it be known he must soon undergo.

"I went down to Black Rock on business, was careful to keep away from the depot, rode thirty miles west after dark and boarded a train there. Dave took a westbound train at Jonesboro, turning back before he reached Memphis, and he was aboard when I got on. Together we came to Kansas City.

"We separated before leaving the train here, he going to the Plaza Hotel, and I coming to the Grand. While on my way here I discovered that some one was trailing me. Later I verified this by leaving the hotel and walking about the town. Always the same man followed not far behind.

I telephoned Dave about my case, and he replied that he had better keep the appointment for me; no one was following him. To that I consented, and you know the result. That, I believe, is all."

It sounded like a lot of bunk, to me—yet there was proof of its reality. Proof lying on my office table, if it had not been removed to the morgue. I knew the Black River country, too, and was willing to concede that most anything might happen there—provided it was bad enough. There were a few questions I desired to ask Mr. Lomax, and I got at them.

"You intended mailing that letter at Black Rock. Why did you change your mind and mail it after arriving here?" I inquired.

"I considered it the safer thing to do. Who knows what means the bandit has for gaining information? He is a power in that district—even a clerk in the post office at Black Rock might be one of his men. I tell you, Mr. Norton, had you been living for a year under the tyranny of the Silent Partner, you would realize—"

"I pass that," I interrupted. "Now, why was there no heading to the letter? Why omit the name of the place where written?"

Lomax's face was a blank for an instant, then it cleared. "I was not aware of the omission," he told me. "Dave wrote it, and he is not very strong on letter writing. Mussel Bend is not a town, and I suppose he simply did not think of putting Black Rock down. That is our post office address."

"I see. Where was the letter written?"

"At my cabin in the hills above my camp. You see, Mr. Norton, I have a daughter, a young woman of twenty, who lives with me. Therefore I do not make my camp my home, as most of the operators do. Dave came up there and wrote the letter."

"Are you sure no one was about when he did so?"

"Absolutely. Except my daughter, of course. Even she did not know what we were planning. Does not know even now where we went, nor what our object was."

"Where is your daughter now?"

"With friends in Black Rock."

"You changed your mind about the time of your departure from Black Rock. Why?"

"In order to have time in which to determine whether we were being watched," was the reply. "Events justified the move—though at a terrible cost. Dave Markey was my best friend."

A good deal that had seemed mysterious in this matter, had cleared up in a perfectly natural way. Maybe the rest of the affair would prove so. At any rate, I made my decision.

"Do you still want me to take this case? Or have you got cold feet, since—"

Lomax got up, his heavy frame towering above me. "I do want you to take the case!" he exclaimed vehemently. "I'll never rest satisfied a single moment, from now on, until I see that devil hung!"

"You're on," I told him. "And we start for the river country to-night."

6

IN THE BLACK RIVER COUNTRY

AT TWO O'CLOCK that morning we boarded a fast train for the Black River section of Arkansas. Besides Lomax and myself, the party consisted of Jim Steel, Bob Mooney, Joe Hilliard and Sticks Bradley, all connected with my bureau. We went in a bunch, occupied a Pullman compartment, and took turns at sleeping.

As a matter of fact, I did not believe Lomax's life to be in immediate danger. The danger passed with the failure to kill him in his room at the Grand.

Why? Because that attempt was not actuated by a desire to kill wantonly, but to prevent him from getting in touch with me. A like motive was responsible for the death of Markey. Of that I felt certain.

I was certain of something else, too. The spies in Kansas City undoubtedly had me spotted. For that reason I decided not to go into the river country under cover. I meant to outwit this Silent Partner person, and do it in the open, since to attempt to work quietly and under cover would in all probability result in disaster.

I had no definite plans as to how I was going to proceed against the crook; time enough for that after I had looked the situation over and gathered further information. But that is not saying I had not some inkling of how to go about establishing the identity of the chief bandit.

That letter, written in Lomax's cabin, looked a very promising clew. For instance, Red Mask must have known its contents almost as soon as it was written, else how could he have known whom the writer meant to consult in Kansas City? How, also, could he have known the real destination of the two operators?

The letter made no mention of Dave Markey, stating only that Lomax would call. It was my belief that Markey's departure for Memphis deceived, just as he intended it to. In fact, his presence in Kansas City probably was not known to the crooks; a belief arrived at from the fact that Lomax was watched while Markey was not.

This is how I sized things up:

A spy stuck to Lomax from the moment he reached the city, while another was watching my offices, ready to act in the event Lomax succeeded in eluding his shadow and reaching them. Probably this second shadow meant to occupy a room in the Mercedes, whence he knew he could have a good view of the corridor outside my door. But the cable-splicer's platform struck him as being surer, safer, and he concluded to watch from there. When Markey came he was recognized and shot down.

Very likely the assassin then got into immediate touch with the shadow set on Lomax, and the attempt on him followed.

I could not, of course, be certain of my conclusions, or any one of them, but in such manner did I reconstruct the thing while *en route* to the field of action.

A lot depended on that letter, and the place in which

it was written. If I could not, by means of it, establish the identity of at least one of Red Mask's gang, then I'd be much surprised.

We reached the little village of Black Rock at noon that day, and a motor boat belonging to Lomax started up the Black River with us at once.

If there were any spies on the platform of the depot when we arrived, they had a lot to report. Every man of my crowd was dressed for his part—simon-pure sleuths from their square-toed shoes to the tops of their Fedoras. I wanted Red Mask to know we'd come—and I was willing to bet he'd soon learn of it.

I'm not trying to weave a shroud of secrecy about the matter. In a nutshell, since I could not "still hunt" this partner person, I meant to hunt him with horn and hounds, as it were. It is my policy, when I think it impossible to creep up on my quarry and trap it, to get it on the run. I meant to start the quarry in this hunt to running.

Twenty miles above Black Rock we struck the lower end of Mussel Bend, and from there on, the west bank of the Black was white with canvas—the contents of the various camps belonging to the master pearlers. They were not continuous, but grouped at approximately one mile intervals, with heavy timber between each location. Back of the tents the Ozarks reared their shaggy, weather-beaten heads. Truly, as wild a section of country as I had ever looked at.

The face of the river, from one end of the Bend to the other, was dotted with the bateaux of pearlers. There they toiled in the hot sun, raising mussel shells from the rocks of the riverbed, each no doubt hoping that this would be his lucky day—the day which would see him forsaking a life of hard work for one of comparative luxury and ease.

They were mining the waters, just as others before them had mined the rocks and ledges of the hills and mountains. They quested for pearls, those others sought gold—all the same in the end.

About midway of the Bend we headed in to shore, ascended a steep path from the river's edge to a high wooden plateau, and found ourselves in Lomax's camp.

It consisted of two dozen small tents, two immense ones, where the cooking and eating was done, and a group of three other small ones in which were housed the foremen, and in which Lomax had the camp office.

We stowed our luggage in Lomax's tent, sought the cook shack, and ate. Night was near, and, besides laying my plans for Steel and his squad, I had a trip to make—one which I desired to have over with before daylight was gone.

7

IN LOMAX'S CABIN

"**HOW FAR IS** it up to your cabin?" I asked Lomax, after we had eaten. "I want to go there as quickly as possible."

"A mile," was the answer, while the operator looked at me in surprise. "What's the idea?"

"Let's go," I replied, getting up.

Lomax led off along a path which climbed a hill through brush and timber, with many huge bowlders flanking it. A mighty good place for an ambush, I thought. Lomax surely was inviting a visitation from Red Mask, passing along that trail day after day. I said as much.

"I have not passed over it alone," he told me. "Not since I decided not to pay the second demand."

"When is that installment due your 'partner?' " I queried.

"Three days from now. Nathan's Rock again is the place."

"Does he always designate that spot?"

"No. He varies it."

By that time we had arrived before a large double log cabin, perched among the bowlders almost on the crest of the hill. We entered a big, comfortable living room, and Lomax, at my suggestion, looked the place over thoroughly in order to determine whether it had been visited during his absence.

"All as it was when I left it," he reported, coming in from the kitchen.

"Now," I said, "bring me the tablet Markey used when he wrote that letter. You have it about?"

"It ought to be here," Lomax replied. "He brought it here for the purpose, being afraid to write in his camp. Yes!" he exclaimed, digging among some papers in a table drawer. "Here it is!"

I took it from him and carried it to a window through which the sun's last rays were coming. There I carefully scrutinized the top sheet—and could hardly restrain an exclamation of gratification at what I saw.

I beckoned Lomax to my side.

"Dave Markey, after the manner of all men unaccustomed to writing letters, bore hard on his pencil while inscribing the one to me," I explained. "Here is a fairly clear impression of that letter—clear enough for a pair of keen eyes to read, especially so just after it was made. That is how Red Mask knew your plans."

I made the statement, startling as I knew it must be to him, in a quiet voice, watching the expression of his face intently.

The man seemed to hear my words, but not to get their meaning.

"Repeat that, will you?" he asked.

I tapped the tablet with a finger. "Some one read this impression, very shortly after it was made, and knew as much about your proposed visit to me as you and Markey did," I told him.

"You say there was nobody present in the house but you, Markey and your daughter. I believe that. Now, think hard and see if you can dig up somebody who came here shortly after the letter was written."

"I don't know of anybody," Lomax answered. "Certainly there was no one here while Dave and I were—wait!" he exclaimed. "Two young fellows came up after the letter was written, folded in the envelope and in my pocket. The tablet, I think, had been placed in the table drawer."

"Now we are getting at something," I applauded. "Who were the callers."

Lomax laughed. "Vin Chadwick and Brady Langdon. Both operators in the Bend. A queer sort of condition exists concerning their calls at this cabin. They are aware that they can come only when I am at home, and, since I am here only infrequently, they make their visits together— Amy, my daughter, being the attraction, of course.

"They hate each other like poison, but are forced to associate for a time, else one yield an advantage to the other. Two nights a week being as often as I think it proper for a young woman to receive company, their opportunities are not many."

Things were working out something after the manner I suspected they might. A sweetheart in the case. Two of them—and therewith a complication.

"Dave wrote the letter after night, then?" I asked.

"Yes."

"Did you two leave the young folks together?"

"Yes. After a bit we went onto the porch and smoked until bedtime."

"During which time," I informed him positively, "one of those chaps read the impression on this tablet. Men are not noted for putting things away after they have used them, particularly at home. They leave that for the women to do. Depend on it, that tablet lay exposed on the table under the light. It was placed in that drawer by your daughter, after the damage was done!"

Lomax was about to voice his astonishment, when a heavy step sounded on the veranda. A second and lighter footstep followed, and a girlish laugh rang out.

"Amy!" cried Lomax, starting up, just as a slim, brown young woman in a very fetching sports costume, ran through the doorway and into her father's arms.

8

TWO MEN AND A GIRL

"**OH, DAD, WHY** did you return to Black Rock and come on here without me?" Amy Lomax demanded, shaking her father in prettily assumed anger. "But I foiled your plot! Made Jimmie Fielder bring me up in his boat—"

"And I took her away from Jimmie and brought her here," came an interruption from the doorway. The voice was deep and pleasant, though not that of a highly educated person, I thought. The speaker came in, hat in hand.

Amy Lomax was pretty enough to hold the attention of any male on this sphere, or any other for that matter, but I was more interested in the man who had escorted her up the hill than in her.

Slightly under six feet high, slim and wiry looking, the young man wore his clothes well—seemed at ease in them. Most any tall, blond young chap of thirty, or thereabouts, looks well in the rough garb common to the out-of-doors, however.

This chap's clothing consisted of a soft, gray flannel shirt with four-in-hand tie to match, gray corduroy trousers, well-kept knee length boots, and a fawn colored Stetson, the latter held in a strong, long-fingered brown hand. His

hair was yellow, eyes blue, and the mouth wide and generous. He wore neither beard nor mustache.

All-in-all, his appearance made quite a good impression on me, and I fell to speculating upon what the other
lover looked like—and which one the blond chap was. His
identity was soon established.

"Brade thinks it a smart trick, stealing a march on Vin—"

"And he only beat me to you by a length!"

Another footstep on the veranda, and the speaker of the
last words stepped through the doorway. He was laughing,
and his face was flushed.

"Vin!" Amy exclaimed gleefully.

"Well, Chadwick," Brady Langdon remarked, eying
the other with a slight frown on his brow, "you're proving
yourself a poor sort of sport. I'd of left you alone, if you-all
had been smart enough to beat me out! "

"It don't make th' leas' bit of difference what you-all
would a done, Brade," Chadwick grinned. "It's mo' to th'
point what I done! I'm lookin' out for Vin Chadwick—
protectin' his interests!"

"Here! Here!" growled Lomax. "You young fellows quiet
down!"

"Let 'em fuss, dad!" Amy begged. "I like to hear it! They
amuse me!"

While they chaffed each other, I took a good squint at
the second comer. Equally as tall as Langdon, Chadwick
was his opposite in all other points of personal appearance.
He was as dark as the other was fair, possessing the black-
est eyes I have ever seen, I believe. Clothed very much like
Langdon, except that his shirt was blue and trousers brown,
while a black Stetson was in evidence in his hand, he did

not present that same spic and span exterior common to his rival.

His clothing showed more signs of wear, and he was not so immaculate either. Still, no denying it, his manner was just as pleasing as Langdon's. The same direct look, the same wide, thin-lipped, generous mouth.

In one other point they differed: Langdon was clearly of a calm temper; one who would take things easy, no matter if the issue should be against him. Would, in fine, not "fly off the handle." A safe man, as I read him. One to be relied upon.

Chadwick, unless his looks were very deceiving, was hot of temper, and restive under restraint or opposition. He was smiling now, seeing that he was highly pleased with the trick he had turned, but I could imagine him exploding wrathfully had the shoe been on his foot instead of Langdon's.

So I read the two men, one of whom I had strong reasons for believing to be in cahoots with Red Mask—a member, in short, of the gang.

Which?

Search me! There were points in disagreement—a lot of them. One was that, should Langdon be aligned with the Silent Partner, let us say, he probably would long ago have framed Chadwick for a killing, thus ridding himself of a rival. And *vice versa*.

Get that? A monkey wrench in the machinery of my deductions already!

"Mr. Norton, daughter," Lomax was saying, and I turned to receive a smiling welcome from Amy, who advanced boyishly with outstretched hand.

"We shall try and make you comfortable, Mr. Norton," she assured me. "If, as I'm taking for granted, you are stopping with us for awhile."

I bowed, then turned to shake hands with Langdon.

"Mr. Norton is a friend of mine from Kansas City, Langdon," said Lomax. "Expects to be here for some time."

"Why not put our cards on the table, face up, Lomax?" I inquired. "Why not tell Mr. Chadwick and Mr. Langdon what my real business is?"

Both men looked at me searchingly, then turned expectantly to Lomax.

"A new operator, come to take the place of one of those the Silent Partner killed!" Amy exclaimed. "I'll bet with you, Brade, or with you, Vin!"

"You'd lose, Miss Amy," I informed her. "I'm a detective, come to lay this Partner party by the heels."

During the ensuing silence I eyed both young men closely, while not allowing either to perceive that I was doing so. I was rewarded in each instance by a blank look.

"Oh!" cried Amy, who evidently was possessed of irrepressible spirits. "A detective! A real, live detective! Oh, Mr. Norton, how funny!"

"Anything but funny!" declared Langdon, laughing. "That is, if Mr, Norton really is here on the job he says he is. Kind of tragic, I'm a-sayin'!"

Chadwick made no comment, simply looking at me steadily, black eyes inscrutable.

Don't you think you'd a did better, Norton," Langdon went on, "if you'd a kep' yore business to yoreself?"

Chadwick nodded a slow agreement. "That's jest what I was thinkin'," he said.

"Wherein you are wrong, gentlemen," I opposed. "I, and my four good men down in the camp, are more than a match for this theatric, sensation-loving, man-killing thief. I am, and by gollies, I'm going to prove it!"

I was strutting my stuff—with a purpose. Was that a smile of derision which for a second parted Chadwick's lips? I could not be sure. In Langdon's face was deep interest, and a look that might have been good-natured contempt.

Both of them baffled me. Then I set off another—would it prove to be a bomb, or a mere fire-cracker?

"Yeah. I come down to get the fellow that dared to have a man killed right under my nose—at my office door," I exclaimed heatedly. "A man that come to me as a client! By gollies, I don't allow no client of mine to be killed, and the killer get away with it!"

"Who—why, dad, who does Mr. Norton mean?" Amy asked in an anxious voice.

I spoke up before Lomax could answer.

"I mean Dave Markey!" I exclaimed. "He's the man that was killed, and all of you know him."

Langdon's eyes closed for an instant, then opened wide upon me, incredulity in their depths.

Chadwick made a slight noise through partly opened lips, and his face slowly drained of color.

"Uncle Dave? Dad!" cried Amy. "It isn't true—it can't be true?"

"Yes, Amy," Lomax replied sadly. "Dave is dead."

With a low cry, Amy Lomax sank into her father's embrace, weeping bitterly.

"Do you-all know what I think of you?" Chadwick

demanded, stepping close to me, his dark eyes flashing sparks of fire. "I think you-all air a damned numskull! Look what you done, breakin' th' news thataway! Detectives? Huh! You air a nut!" He swung about, and walked out of the room.

"For once I find myself plumb agreein' with Chadwick," said Langdon coldly, his blue eyes scornful. "You are all he said—and more. Good night, Mr. Lomax. I'm not goin' to stay no longer, as this ain't no time for outsiders to be around."

He, too, strode out—and left me chuckling, very quietly, in my sleeve!

9

I GET A LETTER

COLD-BLOODED? PERHAPS. ALL in the way you look at it.

Amy Lomax loved her "Uncle" Dave Markey second to her father. I am of the opinion that no matter how the news had been given her, the shock would have been as great, her grief as poignant. So much for Amy.

Now, bear in mind that I was not playing a game of checkers down there in those wild hills. Far from it. I was engaged in a battle of wits, with death as the stake, and the odds greatly against T. Norton.

Two men were in the room, one of whom I was positive belonged to Red Mask's organization, though I had no idea which it was. I wanted to watch the reactions of those men to the sudden announcement of Dave Markey's death. That Miss Lomax should be present was unfortunate.

Justifiable or not, I made the announcement—and got nothing for it. That could not be foreseen. The truth is, I could make nothing of the manner in which Langdon took the news, and likewise drew a blank in the case of Chadwick.

Yet one of those men was in cahoots with Red Mask. Of that I was positive. Was it Chadwick, obviously the weaker of the two, and therefore the more likely to lend himself as a tool? Or was the colder, stronger Langdon the guilty man?

I couldn't make up my mind about Chadwick—and I couldn't quite picture Langdon obeying orders from anybody. So there I stuck.

Lomax, however, thoroughly understood my reason for apparently doing a cruel thing, and approved of it. Miss Lomax went to bed shortly, and did not express herself in the matter.

Darkness had fallen, and I concluded to spend the night in the cabin, there being plenty of room. One reason for staying was that I did not want to leave Lomax alone up there, save for the presence of his daughter. Another was the fact that something seemed to warn me that should I start down that brushy trail to camp I would not see the other end of it. So I stayed.

After I had gone to bed, I chuckled over thoughts of the report the bandit's tool would take him regarding me.

"A blustering, bragging know-nothing!" he would affirm. "No more sense than to announce his business to any and all! Dangerous? Huh! Like a drink of springwater is dangerous!"

And that was precisely the impression I wanted to create in the master mind. It would help me if he believed me to be about half nutty. On the other hand, if he thought me a foeman worthy of his powder and lead, he'd tighten up and stay tight until he succeeded in sinking some of that lead in me.

On the whole, I fell asleep quite satisfied with the day's developments. At least, I had determined the leak through which Lomax's and Markey's plans had trickled into the ears of friend Silent, and I'd made the acquaintance of two

men, one of whom I felt would prove a prominent character in the unfolding of the grim drama which I sensed was
going to be acted—and soon.

Steel and his men had their instructions for the night,
and they had been informed that I might not return to
camp until morning. So I rested easy about them.

I rested easy, too, until morning came. Then not so easy.
A knock on my door at daylight brought me out of bed,
and presently Lomax came in, a serious look on his face,
an envelope in his hand.

"This letter was lying on the front veranda when I went
out this morning, weighted with a rock," he said in grave
tones. "Addressed to you."

He passed it over, and I read the superscription:

MR. TUG NORTON,
       Kaw Valley Det. Bureau.
   By Messenger.

"Is this the handwriting of Red Mask?" I asked.
"The same as in the duns," was the answer.
I took out the inclosure and read:

Headquarters, June 6, 19—.

MY DEAR NORTON:

Glad to have you with us—for a short time. Over night,
let us say. Think, though, that your welcome will be worn to
a frazzle by the time you get this epistle.

Here is my offer—and I never go back on my word:
Leave—and do so before noon today. If you do so, I guaran-
tee you and your party safe conduct. In that I am acting with

customary generosity toward all who obey.

Here is the alternative—and again let me say that I never go back on my word: Remain past the time allowed, and I'll send you to join Markey. That applies to your four men in Lomax's camp. Remember Markey, don't you? Surely.

For reference as to my ability to make good on my threats, and my absolute certainty to do so, I give you any man in The Bend—particularly the big operators.

Short visits are best, my dear Norton—believe me.

Very sincerely,

The Silent Partner.

(Sometimes called Red Mask).

I could not restrain a grin of appreciation when I finished that piece of monumental impudence. What a nerve the fellow had. As a cold proposition, I admired him—hugely!

"I'm afraid you don't take him seriously enough," Lomax complained, after I had passed the letter to him for a reading. "He means just what he says, believe me! Why, look! He knew you were sleeping here last night! Knows, I'm certain, every move you've made since you came! Don't laugh at his threats, Norton! They are not idle words!"

"I take him to be a man of his word, and am not making light of him," I assured Lomax soberly. "He's as bloody a devil as I have ever gone up against. But that doesn't prevent me from admiring his methods and his supreme gall. In the idiom of the vulgarian, he's a whang! Now," I went on, "about this letter. Can you get me specimens of the handwriting of Vin Chadwick and Brade Langdon?"

"Surely, Norton," Lomax objected, "you don't suspect those fellows?"

"One of 'em, yes," I replied. "Don't know which. That's why I want a specimen of their scrawl. Not that I suspect either is Red Mask, but in order to make sure that this letter was not written by either Chadwick or Langdon, or that it was. Both knew my whereabouts last night, but neither could have known my decision to sleep here, unless the trail was watched. I'm pretty sure it was, and closely."

Lomax went out, and I heard him calling Amy. Presently he returned with a couple of folded sheets of paper in hand and offered them.

"Amy is pretty well stocked up with specimens," he grinned. "Here's one from each."

I looked over a note from Langdon first, and passed it up. Not in the least like the writing in the letter I had received. Then I examined the second specimen, that of Chadwick—and drew a second blank.

"These scrawls are those of men not overburdened with education," I remarked. "Not much training in penmanship. Well, it pays to look into these little things as we go along. Now, what are Langdon's antecedents, as known personally to you?"

"Langdon came here two years ago, from Memphis," Lomax replied. "At least, he gave that place as his former home and claims Tennessee as his native State. He had money enough to establish and conduct a pearling camp, so he set in."

"Has he prospered?"

"Apparently. As much as any of us, I think."

"What is his reputation, in reference to his behavior?"

"Excellent."

"Now—Chadwick? What about him?"

"Vin is a native of Tennessee, too. Nashville. But he and Brade were not acquainted back there. That, at any rate, is what both say. He bought a holding in the Bend about a year before Brade came in. However, he got a poorer location, and has had some pretty hard sledding at times."

"Humph! Has he ever had to dig up for his 'partner'?"

"Once. I don't know how he managed, but know that he did."

"What about his habits—all regular?"

"Well, yes—I guess so. Drinks a little and likes to play a stiff game of poker. Nothing bad about him, though, unless you regard what I have told you as being bad. A mighty likable chap, and, frankly, I prefer him to Langdon."

"So. And that brings me to an important question: Which one does Amy favor? Can you answer that?"

He shook his head negatively, his grim features softening into a smile. "That girl doesn't give anything away," he laughed. "Sometimes it looks like Vin has an edge, then Brade is the favorite. Guess nobody knows Amy's mind in that matter, except Amy."

And, I thought, the chances are that she doesn't. I wished, though, that she did, and that I knew which one she really loved. A woman's instincts—a good woman's—are worth taking into consideration in a matter like this.

"Did you ask your daughter about that tablet? Whether she remembers putting it away?"

He nodded. "She placed it in the drawer the following morning, when she tidied up the room," he acknowledged.

"Well," I told him, rising, "that settles that! Vin or Brade—take your choice."

10

LOMAX GETS "ONE"

WE WENT DOWN the trail to camp, after eating a good breakfast prepared by a native woman who served in the house when the owner was at home, and as we were about to depart I noticed a tall native man in the yard. He was about middle-age, and had the hardest-looking blue eyes imaginable.

"Who might be the tough customer?" I asked.

"Meaning Nip Tucker, I guess?" Lomax replied, pointing toward the native. "Well, he's husband to the woman in the house, and is supposed to do chores about the place. In reality, he's a sort of guard I've placed over Amy. Not that I fear harm might come to her from Red Mask or his gang, but because this is a tough country, many men of all kinds drifting in and out. I don't intend for anything to happen to my girl!"

"Certainly not. Are you sure of Tucker?"

"As of myself—more so. Meaning that he's more capable of handling any situation of dangerous nature that may arise than I'd be. He's shrewd, watchful, loyal, and the best shot with a rifle or short-gun in these parts. No doubt whatever about Nip Tucker. I've known him for five years. Bought the cabin I live in from him, in fact."

I took all that with a grain of salt, hoping, of course, that Lomax really knew his man.

Needless to say, we kept our wits about us while we were on our way down the long hillside. We saw no one, however, and reached camp shortly after the pearlers had set in for the day. Steel was waiting for us in Lomax's tent.

"Quite an efficient post office you've got here, Lomax," was the way he greeted us. Then he handed the operator a letter. "Found it on your table this morning."

The operator's face paled as he glanced at the address; then he broke the seal. After a moment he passed the missive to me, and I read:

> Headquarters, June 6, 19—.
>
> My dear Lomax:
>
> You and I have been partners for nearly a year, and this is the first time I have had to complain to you. First time you have showed signs of underhandedness and double dealing. For shame, Lomax! Have I not been fair and square with you? Have I ever demanded more than my share of the profits of our business?
>
> I will answer for you. I have always given you a square deal. Now you are attempting to play crooked with me. You ought to know better! Ought to remember several of my ex-partners who were so foolish as to act as you are now doing. Remembering them, you should be able to cast a fairly accurate horoscope of your own fate, should you persist in holding out on me. It is now only two days until you are due to hand over my share of our profits. Two days in which to come clean. Are you going to do it? Let your answer be upon Nathan's Rock, as per instructions.

If the answer is not there— Now, pay close attention, my dear partner. Something out of the ordinary is going to happen to you; quite different from what has happened to my other crooked business associates. I shall, in the event of your continuing obdurate, strike you where your heart is. Yet you shall live. Ever hear of a man living after he'd been struck center in the heart? No? Well, you shall, unless you get back into the straight and narrow path of business rectitude.

Need I remind you that I never warn but once?

Most sincerely,

THE SILENT PARTNER.

I passed the letter to Steel, making no comment. Somehow, I did not feel like smiling over this letter of Red Mask's, superbly impudent though it was. Instead, the thing cast a sort of gloom over me. He felt so sure of himself, so powerful, so damnably certain that he controlled the situation and held us all in the palm of his hand.

One thing sure, I had a very sincere respect for his abilities. I didn't for one moment think he was bluffing, or that he would fail to do just what he threatened—provided, of course, I could not prevent it.

"You kept close watch over the camp last night, Steel," I said to the operative, when he had read the letter, "that goes without saying. Yet this letter was placed on this table in spite of you. That seems to prove that Red Mask has at least one man planted here. That is not at all a startling discovery, since it is what was already suspected.

"What gets me is this: How did Red Mask, or one of his men, get to the chap who placed the letter here? I am certain it was written after the men knocked off work last night, at about the time another was addressed to me. See anybody stirring around the outer confines of the camp in a suspicious way?"

"They came and went," Steel replied. "Fellows visiting from one camp to another. Things quieted down about eight o'clock, though, and everybody but a few who played cards in a tent, turned in. That was just about dark. We watched all night, and saw nothing unusual."

"One of those visitors from another camp brought the letter in and gave it to one of the gang planted here," I remarked. "That, of course, would be easy. Red Mask acts quickly, no mistake!"

"And appears to be uncommonly well organized," Steel put in.

"What do you make of that threat?" Lomax wanted to know.

"Where is your heart—your deepest affection, Lomax?" I asked suddenly.

The man's face paled. "Why, up yonder on the hill!" he exclaimed. "Amy—good God!"

He stopped there, looking at me with eyes wide with terror.

11

COLONEL BRENT

I NODDED. "THAT is probably what he means to do—strike you through your daughter," I told him. "But get a grip on yourself, man!" I admonished, as he turned swiftly as though about to leave the tent.

"There is no immediate danger to her. Does he not say he will act only in case you fail to leave the money on Nathan's Rock, two days hence? From all I can gather, this crook keeps his word to the letter."

"But," Lomax protested, "you wouldn't have me place absolute dependence in his word, when the most precious thing in my life is threatened!"

"No," I assured him. We shall take extra precautions to protect Amy. After all, he may not be aiming at her. Seems queer to me that he would tip us off to a stunt like that, if he really contemplated doing it. Damned queer.

"May be just misleading us; directing our attention to one point, while he strikes in a totally unsuspected and unguarded quarter. He's subtle, that fellow. But, in any case, don't get excited. We'll see after Amy's safety.

"Hilliard, one of my men, shall reinforce your Nip Tucker, and he will remain at your place night and day. Sleeping days, watching nights. How does that strike you?"

Lomax's face cleared slightly. "That ought to answer," he replied. "I should send her out of here, and at once, only she will not stay away from me. If you think best, however, I'll bring some pressure to bear upon her to that end."

"No. She'd be just as available to Red Mask, if he wants her, in Black Rock as she will be here. On the whole, this is the safest place for Miss Amy, because we can keep a strict watch over her. Now, dismissing that matter for the present, where is Langdon's camp located?"

"The next one below me."

"And Chadwick's?"

"Next above."

"I'm going to pay a few calls," I said, rising. "Will you, Lomax, stick close around camp until I return? My men must get some sleep in order to be fresh for tonight, and I don't want you going about without one of them with you. That goes from now on. I'll see you later."

I stepped out of the tent, and paused to watch the approach of a man who was at that moment coming up from the river. A tall, well set up man in middle life, clean-shaven and showing considerable gray at the temples, I noted when he came nearer.

Like most of the men of means in that section, he wore good clothing, only this man seemed dandified to the point of finickiness. His Stetson was snow-white, and his trousers and belted jacket were of a warm, brown velvet cordu-roy. A diamond blazed in his tie, and he wore gloves.

"Good morning!"

The greeting was cheery and affable, and I bowed, returned his salutation.

"Mr. Lomax about?" he queried.

Before I could answer, Lomax came out, hand extended.

"Well, well, colonel!" he almost shouted. "Back among us once more! Glad to see you!"

"Thanks, Lomax," said the stranger, gripping the operator's hand. "Back again, as you see. Ran down to find out what all this rigamarole about a person calling himself the Silent Partner means. Sounds like a fairy tale. Is there anything in it?"

"I don't know what you have heard, colonel," said Lomax. "But I guess you heard the straight of it. Couldn't be exaggerated." Then Lomax thought of me. "Colonel Brent," he said, "shake hands with Mr. Norton."

We shook hands. "Staying in this country, Mr. Norton?' queried the colonel politely.

"No. I'm a detective. Kaw Valley Bureau, Kansas City," I replied bumptiously. "Came down to lay this Silent by th' heels—and, by gollies, I'm going to do it! Sorry to leave, but I've got business. See you later, and glad to of met you."

I turned on my heel and walked off. On my way out of camp I stepped into a tent where I knew Bob Mooney was sleeping.

"Bob," I said, speaking in low tones after I had shaken him wide awake, "get into your clothes quick. There's a chap over in Lomax's tent, fellow called Colonel Brent. He's your meat. Dig him out. Learn who, what, and all that. Especially where he hangs out and where he's supposed to have been this past year or so. Shake a foot!"

I left Bob dressing, and took my way down to Langdon's camp—though I confess I was not quite so keen on Langdon and Chadwick, now that I'd seen the colonel, and looked into his smoke-gray eyes.

12

A CLEW

ON MY WAY across the mile-wide strip of timber which lay between Langdon's camp and that of Lomax, I got over one mental hurdle that had been troubling me. I had been thinking over the rivalry between Vin Chadwick and Brady Langdon, and it had entered my mind that if Brady, for instance, were in league with Red Mask it would have been an easy matter to frame his rival for a killing, thus leaving the field to himself. The same would, of course, apply in case Chadwick were the guilty man.

The conclusion I reached, and which satisfied me entirely, was this:

Langdon—using him merely for sake of clarity, and not because I suspected him more than the other—was merely stalling about his love for Amy Lomax. Granting he belonged to Red Mask's organization, it would be a mighty fine thing if he were free to come and go at Lomax's home, accepted as a friend.

He could pick up many valuable bits of information—useful in the extreme to his master. As for really being a rival of Chadwick's, he did not, as a matter of fact, care a hoot in the matter.

That course of reasoning satisfied me, and for the simple

reason that it was the only plausible explanation of the thing. I accepted it, and time would prove, or disprove, its soundness.

The only alternative was this: Both Chadwick and Langdon were linked up with Red Mask, and played at being rivals and enemies.

Certainly if both were *bona fide* suitors for the hand of Amy Lomax, either could have got rid of the other and let Red Mask bear the blame.

So, until a better explanation offered, I accepted the only available one, and went forward upon the premises it afforded.

Langdon's camp was a replica of Lomax's, and I was directed to his tent, in which I was told he then was. Halting before the closed flap, I called to him.

"Come in!" came the invitation.

I raised the flap, entered. Then I stopped still, successfully hiding my surprise—I hope.

Across the table from Langdon sat Vin Chadwick, an ugly look upon his face. Langdon's was rather hard and grim, too. Yet they had patently been in close consultation.

Maybe the hard looks were for me. Maybe for each other. I don't know. Chadwick got up, bowed coldly, and walked out of the tent. Langdon waved me to a seat.

"What can I do for the famous sleuth from Kansas City?" he asked with a smile, half friendly and about equally contemptuous.

"Refrain from walking out on me," I grinned, eying the door through which Chadwick had stalked. "Wonder if he'll get up an' leave when I call on him later to-day?"

"What! Going to see Vin, too?"

"Shore. Got to investigate him, same as you."

Langdon gave me a straight, level look from cold eyes. "Say," he exclaimed, "what the devil are you getting at?"

"Oh," I answered, waving a hand airily, "just a matter of form, my dear sir. An investigator has got to investigate all possible suspects. That's all."

Langdon's white teeth showed in a smile, then "burst into hearty laughter. "And I'm a possible suspect?" he asked, controlling himself.

"Sure. So's Lomax. So's Chadwick, an' a lota others I could name. Got to know all of 'em, an'," I leaned across the table and spoke importantly, "it's my opinion that the best way to find out about a feller, is to go right to that feller and ask!"

I sat back, a satisfied smile on my face, and waited to see how he would take that piece of wisdom. To my surprise, his face expressed hearty agreement!

"You're absolutely right!" he applauded. "Go right to the fountain head. Who is in a better position to tell the facts about himself than the subject under the microscope? I'm beginning to think better of you, Norton, old chap, than I did last evening. Now, let's get right down to business. What do you want to know about me?"

I took out a notebook and pencil. "Name, age, height, weight, color hair, color eyes, all marks on body, place of birth, where you vote, married or single—"

"Hey! Stop!" Langdon cried. "Don't shoot so fast, man! You repeat those questions like a parrot!"

I gave him a glare. "Look here, Langdon!" I exclaimed. "Who's doing this, you or me?"

"Go ahead," he yielded. "You're doin' it, of course. But

you-all caint hope to git nothin' outen me, askin' them things like a machine gun shoots!"

I got my questions answered, and a lot more tomfoolery. When asked how many times he'd been in jail, if any, and where his Bertillon record might be found, if anywhere, he lay back in his chair and laughed heartily. I laughed, too—but he didn't know it. I was getting more out of Mr. Langdon that he dreamed of.

"Say," I asked suddenly, "ain't you and that Chadwick on the outs with each other?"

Langdon nodded.

"Then—and remember it's the law which is askin' the question, and answer accordingly—what was he doin' here, gabbin' with you?"

For a moment it looked like Langdon might rise up and throw me out, or attempt to do so at least. Then he grinned.

"I'm going to give it to you straight, Mr. Sleuth," he said, his face sober. "That young squirt came down here and made me a most amazing proposition. He is under the impression that my presence here is detrimental to his interests in a certain quarter. Here's what he proposed: That I sell out to him and leave, or meet him on top of Dead Man's Bald and shoot matters over. Get it? And, getting it, can you beat it or even equal it?"

I grinned. Somehow, I believed he was telling the truth, it sounded so much like what a hot-head like Chadwick would propose. "No," I confessed. "I'll have to pass. What you going to do about it?"

Langdon's face became cold, and the lids dropped over his eyes. Only for a moment, then he looked at me and laughed, "Absolutely nothing!" he declared.

So Chadwick, who was known to have had hard sledding in his business, possessed money enough to buy Langdon out? Odd, to say the least.

I arose and made my departure. "I've got a lot of other investigating to do before night," I told him importantly "Got to be under cover before dark falls. I'm an investigator, not a target!"

I left him chuckling.

Going down to the river I, with Langdon's permission, hired one of his men to row me past Lomax's camp to that of Chadwick.

"Look here, you!" exclaimed that individual, when I pushed aside his tent flap and entered, "git goin', an' do it dam quick! I ain't got no use for you, an' I won't be responsible for whut happens to you if you don't move quick! Git outen my tent!"

I backed out, saying as I went: "You're fooling with the law, young feller! You'll wish you hadn't!"

"I'll kick th' dang law into th' middle of th' Black, if it don't git a move on!" he threatened, starting toward me.

I moved hastily but dignifiedly in the direction of Lomax's camp, leaving the irate operator glowering at me from the door of his tent.

Let him glower! Let Langdon laugh! I'd got a clew, and a good one, at last!

Langdon and Chadwick both appeared to be rather poorly educated, and lacking in polish. Their speech denoted that. Chadwick was genuine. Langdon was spurious, Chadwick, at all times, spoke poor English, and the idioms he used were always correctly used. Even when mad and excited, he rang true.

But Langdon was stalling. At times he used the speech of a well educated person—polished, in fine. At others, when he remembered himself, he fell into the vernacular of the region and bungled his English. And the funny thing about it was that he hardly ever used an idiomatic word as that word should have been used!

Langdon was posing as an uneducated man, while in reality he was anything but that. Why?

Yes, it had been time well invested! Langdon was the man to watch. Of that I was satisfied beyond doubt!

13

AN ENCOUNTER

MY PERAMBULATIONS OF the morning had consumed considerable time, and the sun had passed the meridian when I entered the strip of woods south of Chadwick's camp. Taking a well marked path which skirted the hills and wound among enormous bowlders, I walked slowly along, my thoughts reverting to the man I had met at Lomax's—Colonel Brent.

I considered his polished manner, mode of speech, dress. In those respects he would fit my idea of Red Mask in the flesh. Also, there was something about him that suggested highly tempered steel; a look about the eye that denoted the man of action. Lastly, he had formerly been a fixture in Mussel Bend, but had absented himself for a long period. All that dovetailed to a nicety.

Bob Mooney would have something to tell me about Brent, that was certain. Question was, how much? And of what real value? Time was getting short, and I felt the tingle of big things in the air. Always do, when approaching a climax. Sort of second nature.

Amy Lomax was a problem. I feared to send her away, and I was uneasy with her on the ground. However, I meant to take such precautions as would preclude all possibility

of Red Mask laying his hands on her, powerful and confi-
dent though he be.

Confidence. That was the element in the threat against
Amy that gave me pause. He dared to tip us off before
hand about what he meant to do, for there could be no
doubt that he meant Lomax to understand just what he
was threatening. Could he be throwing a bluff?

He never had done so. Lots of proof of that. Would he
do so now, feeling that things were getting hot and that he
could no longer afford to remain in character?

I doubted it. I've known crooks like him before, and they
invariably take immense pride in doing things according
to Hoyle—their own private edition of Hoyle. No. Red
Mask would not strike before to-morrow night, and then
only in the event Lomax failed to come across.

"But," the thought struck me suddenly, "he won't hesitate
to strike at me!" I glanced at my watch. Half past twelve!
My time limit had passed. How soon might I expect—"

The question was answered before it was fully formed
in my mind!

"Stop!"

The voice came from above me on the west, and I looked
up to see a man, clothed in black, face concealed under a
mask of red cloth. He stood on a ledge of rock which jutted
out from the hillside. In his hands was a rifle—and the
muzzle was trained accurately upon me!

"Get those hands up—quick!"

I obeyed the command instantly, faced about and looked
up at the speaker. I could make nothing of him, only that
he was a man in a red mask. His voice struck no chord of
memory. Was I in the presence of the Silent One himself?

"Well, what's the big idea?" I demanded, careful to keep my arms properly extended. The bandit was not more than thirty feet from me, and I knew he couldn't miss at that distance.

"Any idea what time it is?" came the question.

"Yeah. Half past dinner time," I replied.

"Haven't had your grub yet?"

"No."

"You're going to take an empty stomach into hell with you, then! Pity, because, not having been there, I can't say as to whether the grub is good in that quarter or not. I've heard tell they don't give a fellow anything but hot lead to eat—and I'm going to present you with a light lunch pronto!"

"Why mouth so long about it?" I asked. "What you waiting for?"

"To give you time to realize what a damned fool you are!" snapped the man in the mask—and I saw the muzzle of the rifle grow rigid.

Then I acted. I swung my right hand down, felt the derringer I carried in my sleeve slip into my hand, and the next second the man in the mask was tumbling toward me over the rocks—a slug in his body.

I leaped to where he lay quivering on the rough ground, tore the mask away and looked upon his twitching face. I had never seen the man before. No time to linger there, though. A quick search yielded nothing.

A few minutes later, I reached Lomax's camp, out of breath, and was greeted by the operator at his tent door.

"Where you been, Norton?" he asked. "Got kind of

uneasy about you. Remember what that letter said? Time limit expires at noon?"

"Yeah," I told him, sitting down. "Time limit did expire, and I came damned near expiring with it. Get half a dozen men you can trust, arm them, and let me have 'em for half an hour. Hurry, and don't ask questions!"

A few minutes later I was on my way back to where the bandit had fallen, my escort armed to the teeth. But I might as well have saved the time.

A few spots of blood on the rocks was my only reward. The dead man had been removed.

14

BEFORE THE BATTLE

THE SWIFT REMOVAL of the body of the bandit, doubtless to prevent his face being seen by those who could not fail to recognize him, told me two things. One was that I had been wise to make tracks from the scene just when I did. The other was that the organization of Red Mask was even more highly efficient than I had thought.

Was it the Silent Partner who had fallen a victim to my bullet? No positive answer to that question could be had, of course, but speculation upon the matter was not barred. I thought it unlikely that the bandit chief would bother himself with a little matter like bumping off a numskull sleuth like me. He would, I thought, delegate that job to another.

"At any rate," Bob Mooney commented, when he came to Lomax's tent to report on Brent, "you've drawn blood. That's something."

"Yeah," I answered glumly. "But not enough. What about Brent?"

"Used to be the most prosperous pearl buyer on the river," he replied. "Something over a year ago he announced he'd made his and was retiring. Went away, and, the report is, traveled abroad. Returned this morning unexpectedly.

Has no family, and lives, when here, in a big double cabin at Vincent's Point, five miles above the head of Mussel Bend."

"Humph!" I mused. "A little over a year ago Red Mask began his operations in the Bend—about the same time Brent dropped from sight. Now, just at a time of crisis in the affairs of the bandit, he shows up unexpectedly. Well—"

And there my speculations about Brent ended. I could only guess, and I'd grown tired of guessing. Action was what I wanted. I sought Lomax.

"Have you as many as a dozen men whom you can trust to stand up and fight against the enemy?" I asked.

"Yes," he replied. "There's that many men working for me whom I know well enough to trust. When do you want them?"

"As soon as you can get them together," I replied. "Also, gather up all the arms and ammunition you can lay hands on."

He looked at me, with troubled eyes. "You must be expecting a regular battle," he commented.

"I am," I told him without compromise or reservation. "I've had a sample of how Red Mask keeps his word, or strives to at least. If I'm not greatly mistaken in the man, things will start popping round here to-morrow night. He won't put it off. Thinks you've brought a lot of boobs down here from Kansas City, captained by the father of all boobs—my humble self. Well, all the worse for him."

"What about my daughter?" he queried anxiously. "What plans for her safety have you made?"

"Air-tight," I assured him. "Amy will be safe—no matter what happens to the rest of us."

With that he went off in search of the men he had in mind, and I gathered my bunch around me.

"Hilliard," I said to that operative, "I'm going to assign you to a post of extreme danger. You will go up to Lomax's house and stay there. Sleep days and watch nights. Your particular charge is Miss Lomax. I'm holding you responsible for her safety.

"Man up there by the name of Nip Tucker. Old acquaintance of Lomax's, and trusted in full by him. I guess he's square, but watch him, too. Watch everybody and everything. That's all. You can go up now.

"Steel," I went on, after Mooney had departed, "I'm going to divide up Lomax's men into squads. Four to each side of the camp. Each of you remaining men will be in charge of a squad, and the odd one will be under Lomax.

"Your orders, which you will pass on to your men, are to shoot down any man or men who fail to halt on command. You will take up watch at sundown. I'll make the rounds among you at intervals. Nothing more at present. Better get some sleep, all of you."

Lomax came along presently, and brought the men he had gathered. A fair enough looking bunch. I inspected them and was satisfied.

"You fellows understand what's wanted of you, so there's no need for me to go over things," I told them. "You'll get further orders to-night, and in the meantime you'd better get some sleep. It's to be an all-night watch."

An hour before dark, I accompanied Lomax up the hill to the cabin, and on the way took occasion to caution him against discussing our plans before anybody, even his daughter. Particularly, not before Tucker or his wife.

"I'm not saying Tucker is untrustworthy," I told him. "But the best plan is not to trust anybody any further than you have to. Why, for that matter, I never let even my own men know my thoughts and plans about a case. I give them all I want them to have, and no more. I've found it works fine."

He agreed, and we went on to the house. Hilliard was there on the porch, talking with Tucker, the latter having been ordered to remain at the cabin night and day. Neither had anything to report.

Amy greeted me with friendly cordiality, and while her face still showed traces of grief, her manner was chipper enough.

"Is this callers' night?" I asked her, grinning.

"No," she laughed. "And speaking of that, I'm afraid, dad, that I'll have to arrange to let Vin come one night and Brade another. Otherwise there'll be a ruction here some time. A sure enough ruction!" She was more than half serious—and I agreed with her. Langdon was safe enough in that respect, but, in view of what the latter had told me that morning about Chadwick's proposal, I thought it likely there would be trouble forced by the hothead. Needless to say, I did not reveal any of that to Amy or her father.

My only mission at Lomax's being to see him safely at home, I departed almost immediately. I wanted none of that brushy trail after nightfall—particularly since there was an early moon in prospect. It was risky enough in broad daylight.

Even then, with plenty of light on the path and its surroundings, I carried a six-gun ready in my right hand, and I devoted my senses to watching, rather than thinking.

That is how I came to see Vin Chadwick coming along the trail toward me, when I had covered no more than a quarter of the distance. He was walking fast, head down and hat pulled well over his eyes.

Should I step aside into the brush and let him pass? In all probability he was on his way to Lomax's to put his fate to the test—a final test. Maybe, in his present mood, I'd do well to avoid him. He no longer interested me, save as a possible future son-in-law to Lomax. For that no such hot-head as he would be tolerated by Red Mask, was a firm conclusion in my mind.

On second thought, I decided to risk an encounter, and if I had to bung him up—why, bung him up I would.

I was spared a meeting with him, for, before he was even aware that I was on the trail with him, a shot rang out in the stillness, coming from a point off my right and not more than a hundred yards away. I looked up, caught sight of a puff of white smoke above some brush among a lot of bowlders—and when I turned my eyes to the trail again, Vin Chadwick was staggering to and fro across it like a drunken man. As I looked, he crashed to earth, clawing at the gravel!

15

DOWN THE TRAIL

I DUCKED FOR cover, wishing I had had the forethought to bring a rifle, which would have given me at least a chance of plugging that chap under the brush. Then I circled around until I was beside Chadwick. He was not dead, I soon determined, but had the look of a badly wounded man.

"Well," I said, "here goes!"

The next moment I had Chadwick on my back and was making what time I could up the trail to Lomax's. If the marksman had been convinced that his shot had gone home, he would now be making tracks from the place of ambush. If not, he would be waiting. In which case—

I shivered!

The next moment I heard some one racing down the path toward me, and Hilliard hove in sight. Without a word he slipped his arms under Chadwick's legs, dividing the burden with me, and we hurried on.

"Heard a shot!" he panted. "Thought they'd got you!"

"May have been meant for me, at that," I replied. "No telling."

One thing the shooting of Chadwick did—it decided in my mind, once and for all, who Amy Lomax loved. She didn't go into hysterics, fall on his body and weep. Nothing like that.

She took one look at the face of the wounded man, gasped, closed her eyes, opened them again and started things moving. She had his shirt cut away in a jiffy, her hands steady and her eyes dry. But the look of mortal agony in their brown depths was enough to make one weep.

Chadwick was shot through the left lung—and badly. He came around, after he'd been bandaged and dosed with liquor, but couldn't say anything. He could look, however, and he did—straight into as fine a pair of eyes as ever glorified the face of a woman.

"It's all right, Vin," she whispered. "You're going to live—because I won't let you die! Understand? I won't, because I couldn't live without you!"

I went outside then. I'm too hard-boiled to be present at such tender scenes. Somehow, though, I never doubted from that minute that Vin Chadwick would pull through. The love of a woman can perform miracles!

The nearest doctor was located across the river, three miles above Lomax's camp, at a village beside the ferry. Nip Tucker was already on his way there. But, to my way of thinking, Vin would come through, doctor or no doctor. Amy would attend to that. Hadn't she already said she wasn't going to let him die?

Since I could be of no further service there, and was needed among my men at the camp, I started down the trail once more. It lacked little of nightfall—when that trail was taboo, so far as I was concerned.

Had Langdon shot Chadwick?

That thought kept revolving in my mind, demanding an

answer. For the life of me I couldn't come to any conclusion there. Maybe the would-be killer had mistaken Vin for me, or Lomax; we all were clothed something alike, and Chadwick and I were of a size. Maybe the shot had not been intended for Vin at all. No, sir, I could make nothing of it.

A rattle of gravel attracted me, and I looked up to see a second man coming up the trail. He came slowly, picking his way so as to avoid the worst ruts and the largest rocks.

I stopped, and my gun hand clenched the butt of my revolver.

The man coming along the trail was Colonel Brent!

I was discovered the next instant. Brent looked up, hesitated while he peered through the gathering murk as though in doubt as to my identity. Then he came on more rapidly.

"Good evening!" he greeted, stopping within ten paces of me, quick eyes taking in the position of my gun hand. "You perhaps have just come down from Lomax's?"

"Correct."

"Is he at home?"

"Was when I left."

He eyed me keenly for a moment, then, with a perfunctory comment concerning the Weather, passed me and went on up the trail. I stood aside for him, then watched until his tall form disappeared at a turning.

I made fast time the rest of the distance. Whatever Brent's mission at Lomax's, the operator was in safe hands. I was persuaded, almost, that Brent's hand was in the skullduggery somewhere, but whether as principal or underling I could not determine. But, I thought, if such men as Brent and Langdon are the underlings, what of the leader? He must be something of a super-man!

16

A SURPRISING TURN

ALL WAS QUIET in camp. Steel had his men placed and, in my absence, was making the rounds regularly.

"Select one of your men who knows this district and whom you think you can trust," I bade him. "Send him to me at once, or, rather, bring him." He returned presently, accompanied by a heavy-set native named Wills. I looked him over, decided that he looked square, and called both into Lomax's tent.

"In the first place, Steel, did you see Colonel Brent down here, a short while ago?" I queried.

"Yes. About half an hour since. He inquired for Lomax, then took the trail."

Half an hour ago. That cleared him of suspicion in regard to the shooting of Chadwick. Though he might well have had it done.

"Do you know the location of Brent's house?" I asked, addressing Wills.

"Shore. Vincent's Point. I knows it well."

"We're going up there," I told him. "Are you armed?"

He tapped the butt of a six-gun under his jumper.

"We'll be off then," I said, getting up. "If I'm not back by morning, Steel, you will know in what direction to search. Come, Wills."

I took the stern-seat and the paddle, leaving the native in the bow where he would be under my eyes. I was taking no chances with him. Up the dark, swift river we made our way, passing other boats which slipped silently by in the darkness.

An hour later we stood at the front door of a big, two-story log house, high on a bluff and masked from the river by great oaks and a tangle of underbrush. A lovely spot, with no other dwelling within a radius of three or four miles, as Wills informed me.

The lock on the front door yielded after about three minutes resistance, and we entered a big living room with a wide fireplace at one end. The musty smell of the place betokened long disuse.

Bidding Wills stop by the door, ears open for the approach of the owner, I struck a light and thoroughly but rapidly searched the lower floor, consisting of four big rooms—sitting room, study, dining room and kitchen. Nothing out of the ordinary was turned up.

I went upstairs, accompanied by Wills—and there I found a state of affairs that looked suspicious, to say the least.

The two front rooms contained beds, and those beds had been slept in recently. Moreover, cigarette stubbs and burned matches littered the floors. All windows were carefully masked by means of thick blankets. Another bedroom, in the rear, disclosed a like condition.

The remaining room had been fitted up as a makeshift kitchen. There were dirty dishes on a table against a wall, and considerable canned food stood on a shelf. The room gave every indication of being in use regularly.

And Brent had supposedly been absent for more than a year!

When I got through with that kitchen, as well as with the other rooms, there was no nook or cranny I had not peered into. But nothing more damaging than the fact that the rooms were in use when supposedly vacant was learned.

"Guess that's about all we can do," I said to Wills, not quite able to keep the disappointment I felt out of my voice. "We've learned something—"

"There's one place you ain't looked yit," he broke in. "That air chimbley cupboard." He pointed to where the chimney came up through the floor on its way to the roof. "Mos' chimbleys has a cupboard. This'n mought have."

I was at the chimney in a jiffy, but it required considerable searching before I found what I sought. Finally a loose nail came away in my fingers, and a door which extended from floor to ceiling swung open.

I'd found what I sought!

On shelves in the cupboard were many boxes of cartridges, rifle and revolver, while a dozen rifles were stacked far back in a corner. The most damaging thing there, however, was this:

A roll of red calico—red like the mask worn by the bandit I had slain on the hillside that day!

I closed the door, inserted the nail, then turned to Wills.

"We'll be going," I told him, my voice somewhat shaky in spite of me. "Chances are some of the gang will be here before the night is much older—and we pointedly do not want to be found. You first."

We were presently on the back trip, and going rapidly with the current.

"Brent!" I kept exclaiming in my mind, over and over. "Brent is the Silent Partner!"

Then my thoughts reverted to Langdon. Could it be possible that he was entirely innocent? Might not some one else have seen that tablet right after Markey wrote the letter?

I asked the question—and the answer came with the suddenness of a stroke of lightning.

"Tucker! Nip Tucker! Why not he? Without doubt he was on the premises when Dave wrote the letter. Why not Tucker in the role of accomplice, rather than either Chadwick or Langdon?"

I reached camp the most sorely puzzled sleuth who ever wore a shield!

17

ASHES AND MYSTERY

UPON RETURNING TO camp I immediately dispatched Steel and Wills to the vicinity of Brent's place, with instructions to keep hidden, and watch. One or the other would report to me the following day.

Then began the tedium of night patrolling. Once every hour I visited my outposts, and between times I tried to unravel my tangle.

Brent, as I saw it, had conceived the idea of laying tribute on the big operators. To that end, he had announced his retirement, giving it out that he would spend some time abroad. He had remained in the country, instead. Doubtless he had perfected his organization before dropping out, and had it ready for action immediately.

That his house had been in use only as a get together place when a raid was to be pulled, was my conviction. The real place of Brent's concealment probably lay far back in the hills, perhaps in one of the numerous caverns of which the country boasted.

Everything pointed to Brent. Brent, with Nip Tucker, he of the hard eyes and deadly marksmanship, as an able accomplice having the confidence of Lomax, one of the leaders of the big operators.

Should I take Brent in at once?

Judgment interposed an objection to that. What could I prove on the handsome colonel? Absolutely nothing. It is true that, granting I was right in my suspicions concerning him, he would be unable to prove an alibi in so far as his announced European journey was concerned. But what matter? The burden of proof would be on me. I would have to do the proving, not he.

No. The only way in which to bring Brent's guilt home to him was to take him red-handed. That was it.

The night passed without incident worthy of note, and just as dawn was breaking Steel and Wills came up the trail from the river—excitement speeding both of them. Steel beckoned me into the tent, and Wills was right on my heels.

"When we got to Vincent's Point," Steel reported, his voice heavy with suppressed excitement, "we found Brent's house just tumbling into ruins. It is now ashes!"

That was a blow between the eyes, and no mistake!

"Yeah," seconded Wills, "ashes. We seed th' flames afore we got thar, but couldn't decide whether it was a brush fire or a house. It war th' house!"

"Any sign of the colonel?" I asked quickly.

"Nary a sign," Wills replied.

"Anybody else?"

Steel shook his head in a negative.

Dawn had come. Summoning Steel to follow, I took the trail to Lomax's on the run. Arrived there, my first question was of Brent.

"He left here about nine o'clock last night," Lomax said. Went down the trail toward my camp, on his way back home. At least, that is where he said he was going. What's happened?"

"House burned last night," I replied shortly. "What did he come up here for?"

"Said he wanted to confer with me about something," Lomax replied. "But when he saw what a state things was in, the doctor being here by then and all hands busy, he went away. Said he'd see me first thing in the morning."

I considered for a moment, then said:

"As you value your own life, and the safety of your daughter, do not divulge one word of our plans to Colonel Brent when you see him. Don't ask me why, just heed my warning and keep it to the letter. Now, how is Chadwick?"

"He rested well last night, under opiates, and seems to be bright enough this morning," he reported. "It's going to be nip and tuck with him, but doc says he's got a fine chance—with good nursing."

"He'll pull through, if the nursing will do it!" I grinned. "Come on, men. Our day has just begun!"

Back in camp, I called in some of Lomax's men from the river and set them to cutting trees, sawing them into logs, and to gathering all the down wood they could find. Under Steel's supervision, the wood, when brought up, was made into huge piles in a circle about the camp and in the edge of the forest which in no place approached closer than a hundred yards to the tents.

Also, I dispatched two men to Black Rock in a fast motor boat, with instructions to bring back as much coal oil as their boat would carry without danger of swamping.

That fire at Brent's had given me an idea. I meant to use it for all it was worth.

Lomax came down the hill while I was in the midst of those activities, and I never saw a more puzzled man in my life.

"Just leave things to me," I told him, in answer to his questions. "I'm getting ready for trouble. It may come to-night—probably will. Haven't changed your mind about coming through with that ten thousand, have you?"

The operator's face grew red. "I'll lose everything I've got, even my life, before I'll yield one damn dollar!" he almost shouted, as he turned squarely about and stalked into his tent. Lomax's nerves were getting jumpy—as well they might.

By noon I had begun to wonder more and more about Brent. He should have been down long before, telling us about the fire that destroyed his house. He failed to show up.

I woke Wills, poor devil, and sent him up there. At three o'clock he came back with the news that, while a number of natives had gathered about the ruins, no one had seen the colonel.

Now what? I couldn't get that curve at all! What was his game? Had he decided to get out of the country, destroyed his house and the evidence it contained?

I dismissed that idea. Colonel Brent might be as black as the devil himself—but he hadn't the earmarks of those who run. No. He'd make a last stand, no matter what the odds. A quitter? Absolutely not!

18

UNEASY HEADS

JUST BEFORE NIGHT I had the circle of wood heaps soaked in coal oil, and instructed Steel to light every other one. Once started, those heaps of logs and brush would burn until daylight at least. If Red Mask sent his men into the clearing past those lighted heaps—well, he'd lose 'em. That was that.

During the day, Steel had recruited half a dozen more men whom he picked from the crowd. "They'll stick, I think," he told me. "Lomax has promised them all big pay, just as he did the others. The best I can do, anyhow."

With five of the new men and Wills, I went up the hill to Lomax's place, starting just after night had fallen. From then on until the end, my place would be on the hilltop. Steel had command of the camp.

Lomax, being a fighting man, remained down there. I insisted on that. Didn't want both birds in the same nest. Too easy for Red Mask, and he might take advantage of it by concentrating his attack on the house.

Hilliard and Tucker were stationed inside the house. I didn't want Tucker free to prowl around. Inside, I'd make sure he didn't get out.

Miss Lomax seemed undisturbed by our suggestive

activities, being wholly taken up with ministering to the wounded man, who seemed to be doing nicely.

My six men were scattered in the brush in a circle about the cabin—with instructions to shoot any man who tried to cross the clearing, after he had been ordered to stop.

With a keen ear for sounds of battle from the camp below, I settled down to watch. Nothing happened, either in camp or at Lomax's cabin. Day found us red-eyed, sleepy and, to tell the truth, disappointed. I confess I wanted the thing over with, and I suspect all concerned felt about it as I did.

Just before I started with my squad for the camp, Brady Langdon came up the hill.

"Heard about Vin's mishap yesterday," he said, after eying my men critically, even wonderingly, and greeting me. "Sorry he got in the way of a bullet. Wouldn't be at all surprised if he got a dose meant for you, Mr. Sleuth. Eh?"

"Might of been."

"Is the guard for Vin, or what?"

"We been rabbit huntin'," I told him shortly. "You'll find the folks you want to see—in the house!"

I left him standing on the trail, laughing.

All was quiet in camp, and, after gathering another supply of wood, my night-hands turned in. Nothing had been heard of Colonel Brent, and since he had no known relatives in the vicinity, we had no idea where to inquire.

I turned in, too, and slept until well into the afternoon.

When I awoke I set out upriver for Brent's place, only to learn that he had not shown up there. The information came from a native Steel had hired to stay on the premises and notify him the moment anything was learned about the missing owner.

As for Colonel Brent, I'd settled the mystery of his disappearance to my own satisfaction. Either he had decamped, or was going to directly after making good his threat against Lomax.

That night passed as had the one before. Likewise the next and the next. Every man of us was noticeably shaky. Insufficient sleep, coupled with the constant strain of suspense, was telling on us.

Would Red Mask strike, or wouldn't he? I began to suspect that he was purposely delaying matters in the hope of demoralizing our forces through the ravages of uncertainty.

On the fifth night I decided to offer him a little bait. Maybe he would bite. I caused it to be known that we were resting easy about things, and that only a small guard would be put out from then on.

"Red Mask has got cold feet," I was quoted freely as saying. "When he found out what he was up against, he pulled his freight!"

That night no fires were lighted. Instead, I had caused to be made upward of two hundred cotton balls; these were soaked in kerosene and placed at strategic points about the camp, each pile being guarded by one man, and instructions were to light them and hurl them in the direction of any attacking point. My men were barricaded behind logs, and I hoped to cause sufficient illumination with the balls to enable them to shoot at something besides shadows.

Again we passed a peaceful night.

"What do you think, Lomax?" I asked the operator, just before darkness fell on the sixth night. "Has he quit?"

He shook his head negatively. "Not he," was the reply. "Just waiting for a good chance."

He was. That night he struck.

19

LEAD FLIES

SO CERTAIN WAS I that that sixth night would tell the tale, one way or another, I sent Steel up to Lomax's and remained in camp. I felt safer about things up there. The camp presented so many points of easy attack, I knew we would have a hard time repelling Red Mask's men when they came—if, indeed, we should be able to do it at all.

I had just started for Lomax's tent, at about eleven o'clock that night, when the first warning came.

"Halt!"

The challenge was on the south side of the camp, toward the hills.

The reply was a crash of rifle fire, followed by shrill yells such as a band of Indians might have taken pride in.

Another volley split the air, that from my own men, and the next minute I was with them.

W–h–h–h–i–i–i–z–z–z–z–z!

A fire-ball sailed over my head and landed in the clearing near the rim of trees. It was followed quickly by another and still another.

In the light thus created I caught sight of several slowly advancing men, all in red masks. I picked out one and let drive. He threw up his hands and fell backward.

Other men, from the remaining posts, came on the run, shooting at the dodging figures faintly disclosed by the fire-balls.

Other oil-soaked wads of cotton followed the first, the dry leaves and twigs among which they fell took fire, and all the while my men were firing steadily.

Suddenly all grew quiet. Not an enemy was to be seen. Then the lone man left on guard at the north side of camp got into action with his rifle.

"They're coming at us from the north!" I yelled, and led my crowd in that direction.

But the fire-ball man was there ahead of us. By the time we got within shooting distance, we had targets to shoot at.

Again the night was made hideous with crash of rifle and revolver, wild yells, groans and shrieks. Fire-ball after fire-ball sailed above us and far into the clearing—and again we won.

The attack ceased as suddenly as it had begun, and this time the defeat was decisive. An hour passed, and then we began to look the field over.

Five dead. Such was the toll we took of Red Mask's gang that night. We brought them in and stripped the masks off the faces of those who had not themselves torn them away in the agonies of death.

"This'n is from Chadwick's camp! Lem Taylor! I knowed him well!"

"Another one frum Chadwick's!"

"Here's one from Bailey's!"

"Peck Ridley, or I'm a liar! He's front Langdon's!"

Such were the cries of recognition when all faces were bared.

"Scatter and see if we can bring in one wounded!" I ordered. "Then maybe we can get the straight of things!"

But there were no wounded—else all such had been taken away by their companions.

"I'm off for your place, Lomax," I told the operator. "Stay right where you are until morning—and watch, all of you."

I reached the edge of the clearing on top of the hill, and was met by Steel.

"Lord!" he ejaculated. "You must have had one hell of a ruckus down there! "

"Right smart fight," I told him. "We lost one man outright, and got three wounded, none badly. Knocked over five for them. How's things up here?"

"All quiet!"

As though to give him the lie, at that moment there came a dreadful cry from inside the house. We looked for an instant into each other's eyes, then raced for it.

The door to the living room was locked, but I sent it crashing inward—and almost stumbled over Chadwick, from whom the cry had come and who was trying to crawl outside. I bent over him, saw that his bandages had been torn away and that he was bleeding copiously.

"Steel!" I cried. "Look to Chadwick! I'll take care of the rest!"

In the kitchen, on his hands and knees, in an effort to struggle to his feet, was Hilliard, a bleeding wound on the back of his head.

"What's happened?" I cried, helping him to rise.

"Don't know!" he mumbled. "Was sitting—in chair—in here. Somebody hit—me. That's all—I know!"

Into the remaining rooms I rushed—to discover nobody!

Then I fell to cursing myself fluently. Tucker! Hard-eyed Tucker! He was the traitor!

Ten minutes sufficed to establish the fact that nobody had entered or left the house across the clearing in any direction. My men were certain of that—and I was almost certain there was no traitor among them.

But Amy Lomax was gone. That was certain. So was Tucker and his wife. Where, and how, had they gone?

Then, standing in the kitchen where Hilliard had been struck down, my eye caught a slight inequality in a bit of flooring in the corner beyond the stove, and I had it up in a jiffy.

A trapdoor! Cunningly concealed and its existence known only to Tucker and his wife, in all probability!

"Hell!" I shouted aloud. "Of course! Lomax bought the place from Tucker! No wonder Red Mask was so certain he'd be able to get hold of Amy!"

A ladder led downward, but before I descended I called Steel to me. "How about Chadwick?"

"I think we were in time," he answered. "He managed to whisper a few words. Says a man in a red mask came into the room, not over half an hour ago, and, without a word, tore his bandages off and threw them on the floor. He fainted, then, but says it was for only a moment as he heard a scuffling sound in the adjoining room where Amy was. Then he started crawling out to give the alarm. It was he who cried out."

"Good boy!" I applauded. "Well, I won't be far behind them. This is a crevasse, I think, and probably runs under the hill to an outlet not far away. As soon as you can get away, gather the men and follow me. So long!"

I had sworn to Lomax that his daughter was in no danger, and I vowed not to face him again until I could give her safe into his hands. Down the ladder I went, struck bottom within a few feet and found myself facing a crevasse in the rock, just as I had predicted to Steel.

With a gun in one hand and a flash light in the other, I stepped within the dark passage, and struck out over its rock-strewn floor.

20

THE BLACK PATHWAY

THE FLOOR OF the crevasse had an upward trend, and fifteen minutes after I entered it I came to an outlet in the side of the hill back of the cabin, half a mile distant. The exit was completely masked by bowlders and brush, a tight squeeze for any person to pass through.

What next? I knew that Amy and her captors could not be far ahead of me, and, lacking anything positive to go on, I descended the hill along a shallow gully which led to the valley and into deep timber. That was the easy mode of descent, and I figured they had taken it.

At the foot of the hill I came upon confirmation of my opinion. A white handkerchief lay beside a bush just at the edge of the wall of trees. I picked it up, put it in my pocket, and prayed that the girl would have presence of mind enough to leave other signs of her passage—a hope I was not to realize, however.

Dawn found me still beating the brush far to the west, in the direction I knew the party had headed when they came into the forest. I had seen no one, nor had I come across a human habitation. No sign of Steel and his men, either. They had no doubt gone off in another direction.

The sun was well up when I came upon a boy fishing on

the shore of a lake, and I frightened him nearly out of his wits when I accosted him.

"How long you been here, son?" I demanded, coming up beside him.

The urchin leaped up, dropped his pole, and started to run.

"Don't run!" I begged. "I'm not going to hurt you! How long have you been fishing here?"

"B-bout a n-nour!" he gulped.

"Seen anybody pass here?"

"N-no, sir!"

"Any houses around here close?"

"Jist pappy's. We lives a mile nawth."

"Who is at your pappy's house now?"

"Nobuddy but him an' mammy an' th' younguns."

"Mighty lonesome sort of a community," I observed. "Sure there's no other houses close?"

"W-well, thar's th' old Hankins place, two miles beyond th' head of th' lake," the youth remembered. "It air empty, though. Nobuddy lived th ar th' las' five year. No folks wants to live that fur away frum things."

It was a chance, and I decided to take it. "How do you get to the Hankins place?" I asked.

"Foller yore nose right up th' bank of th' lake, this side, ontel you-all come to th' end of it. Then turn right ontel you come to a old rail fence. Then you air thar."

"Good. Here's half a dollar, and if you'll take a note to Mr. Lomax's house for me I'll give you another half, and then a whole dollar when I pass this spot again—about to-night. If I don't see you here I'll leave it under the rock you are sitting on. Is it a trade?"

"You bet!" cried the boy, leaping up.

I scribbled a line to Steel to tell him where I had gone. That was all. The boy took it and was off on what must have been a fifteen mile hike.

Half an hour's walking brought me to the head of the lake. There I struck off to the right and reached a corner of rotten rail fence, approaching it through dense brush. I stopped and took a long look.

Across a sea of sprouts I could see the roof of a cabin, with a stick-and-mud chimney—and smoke was curling lazily from it!

Empty, the boy had said. Well, somebody had moved in. That was sure.

I got over the fence and crawled through the brush, going slowly and with extreme care, until I was close enough to get a view of the front door.

There, with his chair tilted against the wall, smoking a pipe in peaceful enjoyment, sat a familiar figure—Nip Tucker, in fine!

I had run my game to cover!

Then I grew suddenly suspicious. Why had they gone into a hole so soon? Did not they realize that the whole country would be scoured? Surely.

A solution of that point came on the heels of the first thought. Amy. She could not travel fast over such rough going. That was one item. Item two: Red Mask had returned to learn what fate had attended the attack on the camp, gather his men, and retire to the real stronghold, which no doubt lay farther back in the hills.

He had counted, no doubt, on a long lead; figured that Amy's absence would not be discovered until daylight. It probably never entered his head that there was enough life left in Chadwick to enable him to give an alarm, and he or Tucker had finished off Hilliard, as they thought. Joe's head, however, was hard.

Whatever the explanation, Tucker sat there in front of me, and I felt sure Amy was inside. Amy and Tucker's wife, perhaps. The next move was to get her out, and do it without delay.

To my right, and beyond the cabin, I could see a small stable, and I gained its cover. From inside the stable I could get a view of the rear of the house. It had no door nor windows.

Should I creep up, shoot Tucker—

I broke off, staring hard at a man who was approaching across the clearing—a native, by the look of him. He passed from view in front of the house, and I passed up the idea of creeping up on Tucker.

Then a possible chance occurred to me. In a sort of crib beside me was a lot of litter, moldy hay and corn stalks. That stuff would burn nicely—and a native's nose is keen for fire.

I struck a match, dropped it into the litter, watched until certain it had caught, then ducked through the brush toward the upper side of the cabin. There, a dozen yards from the door, concealed by the undergrowth, I waited.

21

THE SILENT PARTNER

I HAD NOT long to wait. Even my untrained nose told me there was a fire burning somewhere, and pretty soon Tucker came to the door, sniffed the air, walked to the corner of the cabin, then called excitedly:

"Hey, Wallace, th' crib's on fire! Come a-runnin'! It'll spread, an' thar'll be hell to pay!"

The man called Wallace ambled out and the two ran for the barn. The next minute I was inside the cabin—confronted by an angular woman whom I knew as Mrs. Nip Tucker.

I gave her no chance. Before she could cry out, I had her on the floor, had torn her apron off and gagged and bound her. Then, with no ceremony whatever, I rolled her under the bed as far as I could put her.

Then I looked up to find Amy Lomax, tied to a chair, but thoroughly alive to the situation.

"Mr. Norton!" she cried. "How did you find me? How many are with you? How is Vin? Oh, I'm afraid he killed Vin!" she began sobbing.

"Who?" I demanded.

"I d-don't know," she wailed. "The man in the mask! He came part way with us, then turned back. Said he'd join us here "this morning—but he hasn't come yet. About V-Vin? How—"

"He's O K," I assured her, as I cut her bonds. "See that ladder?" I asked, pointing to one in a corner which led up to a manhole in the loft.

She nodded.

"Well, you get up there quick!" I ordered. "Business is going to pick up around here pronto, and I want you out of the way! Hurry!"

Without a word of protest, she climbed the ladder and disappeared in the dusty, cob-webby loft. I ventured outside and took a look around the corner of the house.

I was just in time.

The fire had gained too much headway, and the natives were returning to the house. I stepped inside, took my six-gun by the barrel and waited.

"Who in hell could of sot it? I ain't been near thar!"

"Spark from th' chimbly, like as not."

"Yes, I reckons."

The two men were almost at the door.

"Come on in," said Tucker. "You-all must be hungry. Th' old woman will git you up a snack."

His tall form loomed in the doorway, he crossed the sill—and I struck with all I had. The manner in which he fell convinced me he would not get up again.

An oath from the man outside, then running footsteps. I sprang over Tucker and out of doors. Wallace was running for the brush—and I got him at its edge.

Without loss of time I ran to where he lay and dragged him into the weeds until his body was concealed from view. Then I hurried inside.

"Amy!" I called. "Come down! We've got to— No! Stay there!"

Some one was coming through the weeds toward the house! I wheeled to the door—and faced a man on the sill. He wore a blood-red mask!

Both went for our guns at the same moment, and mine spat flame a split-second before his got into action. When I fired I leaped aside, crouched into a corner, and let drive again.

The tall man in the mask wavered in the doorway, his gun arm limp beside him. After one tremendous effort to raise the weapon, he let it clatter to the floor—then pitched forward on his face.

I ran outdoors, made sure he was alone, then came back, called Amy, and turned him over. My fingers clutched the mask, and I hesitated. Whose features lay hidden there?

I gave the thing a yank.

"Langdon! Good God!"

Amy was beside him in a flash, kneeling down. "Brade!" she cried. "Oh, Brade! What does it all mean?"

As though her voice had recalled him, the dying man opened his eyes and spoke.

"Put—something under—my head," he begged. "I want—to talk."

"Wait!" I exclaimed. "Get away, Amy! As long as that reptile has life in him he's liable to bite!"

The man on the floor gave me a look of scorn. I snatched the girl away, nevertheless, took a derringer out of Langdon's sleeve and another six-gun off his hip, then I put a pillow under his head and made him comfortable. If he wanted to talk, I was willing. He wouldn't have long. A man shot through the stomach in two places ain't apt to do much talking.

"You—win, Norton," Langdon said, his voice low, but distinct enough. "Partly—because I took—you for a—dumb head. When—I got back—found out yu'd—wiped out my—gang, almost. Rest of th—damned cowards had scattered. A poor lot—as it—turned out. Damn 'em!

"Haven't got long," he went on. "Want—to tell—you a few things. Save—a lot of—bother afterward. You got—the man—that killed Markey. Chap—you killed when—he should—have got—you. As for Chadwick—that—bullet was—meant for you. I guess—I finished him—last night. Hope so. I—knew I couldn't—have Amy. Planned to—take her by—force. Give her—back to—Chadwick—when I got—through with her—if he'd care to have her—then."

A low moan from Amy, as she covered her eyes with her hands. Langdon was being frank, to say the least.

"He got in—way—of that—bullet, so I—decided—to finish him. Guess I did. Hope—so."

"You didn't, though," I broke in. "Had you done so you might have got away with this thing. He gave the alarm and put me on the trail right after you left. Vin is going to make a life of it, and that's that!"

"No matter. I had—a lot of—fun while it—lasted. More than when I—was on the—stage. By the way—I'm ambidexterous. Wrote that letter to—you with—left hand. Pretty clever—eh?" He laughed.

"What about Brent? Know what became of him?" His time was short, and I wanted him to get on.

"If—you'll watch—the sky, north of the—trail from Lomax's to his camp—the buzzards will show—you where—he is. What's left—of him. Burned his—house. Hid evidence. Old fool came nosing—into things. Talked to Lomax. He paid. Any questions—you want—to ask? Hurry! I'm going!"

"The money you've robbed and killed for? Where is it?"

A horrible grimace spread over Langdon's face.

He laughed—a gush of blood came from his lips.

That was all. He died without another word.

The breath was hardly gone from his body when Steel, Lomax and half a dozen men arrived at the cabin. They had met the urchin shortly after he left me.

Lomax, after holding his daughter close for a long moment, and assuring her that Vin was going to get well, turned to the man on the floor.

"Langdon!" he ejaculated. "Langdon—of all men!"

I nodded. "Yep: Fooled me too."

"The Silent Partner? Langdon the Silent Partner?"

"Yeah. Damned silent," I answered, as I walked out doors for a smoke.

LOST LAKE

From the Jungle Green of the Desolate Forest,
I Looked Out Over the Bosom of the Water,
Doomed, I Thought, Ever to Remain a Waste

1

INTO THE HINTERLAND

WHEN THE NEW police commissioners looked the bunch over at headquarters in Kansas City, and subtracted from the force all those politically off-colored, I spent about one day indulging a sense of undeserved injury. Then I woke up and started sleuthing on my own.

I am not averse to self-advertising, since my business depends a lot on getting itself before the public in a favorable light, so I have no blushes to cover up when I say that the Kaw Valley Detective Bureau has been in the limelight ever since. Furthermore, I, Tug Norton, founder, owner and chief operative of the bureau, have not failed to gather unto myself a goodly store of shekels and a thoroughly pleasing publicity. Some call it fame.

All of which merely prefaces this:

Success in the private sleuthing game brings not only considerable responsibility, but carries a full measure of danger along with it. Many of my cases, of course, have not possessed the element of personal risk, but most of them have bristled with it.

It is one of the latter kind I now have in mind. When I ventured into the wilds on this particular case, I was not unaware that things were going to prove hot—but I never

*Just as I drew bead on Blackhead's thigh—a
negro appeared at the door, gun in hand.*

suspected just how hot they would be before I came to the
end of the trail.

Torrid. That expresses my notion of the temperature,
wholly man-made and governed, of the place when I
entered it—even before I was in it. And all over a lake.
Lost Lake.

George Van and his sister, Rita, sent the summons. It
was exactly that—a summons. The letter did not ask me
to consider the case and advise whether I would undertake it. Not at all. George and Rita were not that kind.
They needed a detective; had heard of me and the Kaw
Valley. That was sufficient. They wrote for me to come—
sending along gilt-edged bank-references, and stating
that money was no object to them, so long as they got the
service required.

That sort of statement commands my respect, and
usually enlists my undivided activities. The bank reference
stood up—and George and Rita were promptly advised
that they had bought themselves one sleuth.

The summons, in letter form, ran as follows:

Kirkland, Mo., June 12, 19—.

T. Norton, Mgr., Kaw Valley Bureau,

    Sandstone Bldg., Kansas City, Mo.:

Dear Sir—A reference to any one of your local daily papers, of a month ago, May 12, to be exact, morning issue, will inform you concerning the known facts surrounding the mysterious death of Roger Van. You will note, among other items, that he was found dead on the lower terrace of Rockaway Place, his home in the hills on the shore of Lost Lake, and that he died from a wound caused by a rifle bullet fired into his body by a party, or parties, unknown.

Roger Van was my father, and a retired merchant who chose to build his home in a wilderness, and to rear his children there. There are two children, sole representatives of the family now. Myself and my sister. Rita. We are at present living at Rockaway—in a state of uncertainty and fear.

Referring you to the morning issue of the Kansas City *Sun,* May 15, last, you will note that the consensus of opinion among the officers who investigated the circumstances of my father's death, was that a stray bullet from the rifle of a hunter in the vicinity of the place probably was responsible. There were no known enemies, and no motive for the killing could be unearthed. No robbery was committed. There the matter of my father's death rests to-day.

My sister and I did not agree with the authorities at the time, nor have we since gone over to their side. On the contrary, we are more than ever convinced that father was murdered in cold blood—and that we will be, and very soon, unless the murderer of Roger Van and the would-be assassin of his two children is promptly taken and confined.

Two attempts, Mr. Norton, have been made on the lives of my sister and myself. One occurred a week ago, and was aimed at me. A shot fired from a far hillside, in the early morning when I stood on the upper terrace. It missed, but broke a window just back of me.

The second attempt involved the use of dynamite, and it was only by the merest chance that Tango, our Negro servant, discovered the sputtering fuses and extinguished them before they had time to reach the cache of explosive—ten sticks— under the bedroom wing of the house. The hour was eleven o'clock, and sister and I had retired. Tango, who sleeps on the ground floor, was aroused by noises outside, and investigated. That occurred three days ago.

My father left my sister and me very well off in the matter of worldly possessions, and we are prepared to spend the last dime of our inheritance, if necessary, to run down and punish his murderer, to say nothing of preserving our own lives.

We are situated at considerable distance from what you might term the "beaten track," and I shall here give explicit directions whereby you may come to us.

Board the local passenger on the C and A, east-bound, and

get off at Kirkland. Cross the river there, by skiff, and inquire
at fisherman's shanty for the most direct trail to Lost Lake.
Three miles up the trail into the hills, you will find the cabin
of a farmer, Trout, and there you may procure a horse for the
balance of the journey. It is ten miles farther to the southern
extremity of the lake. We live on the opposite bank to that
upon which your horseback journey will terminate, but there
will be no difficulty in getting a native to put you across.

We shall expect you, Mr. Norton, within three days at the
outside, and would appreciate an earlier arrival.

For reference as to our financial standing, you may inquire
of Mr. Walter R. Hammar, president of the Miners' and
Merchants' National Bank in your city.

Yours very truly,
GEORGE VAN.

How did I react to that letter? Favorably. I had resolved
to confine my activities to cases within the city, but what
could I do? There was something in the plight of that lad,
George, and his sister, that enlisted my sympathy. All alone
in that old pile called Rockaway Place, of which I had
heard, and in deadly danger from forces with which they
were poorly equipped to combat.

It is just as much the business of a sleuth to help people
out of trouble as it is to get troublesome people into more
trouble. I elected to help George and Rita.

2

A LEAD COMB

GETTING OFF THE train at Kirkland was the only easy, uncomplicated part of the journey. The village was no great shakes, serving as it did a very poor farming community. A store or two and a few dwellings of mean character. A negro fisherman rowed me across the Missouri, and I landed on a bit of table-land which lay like a very small portico before a gigantic and rambling mansion—the mansion being the hill which rose majestically and abruptly back of it.

A scrawny, dirty, bewhiskered native who lived in a sort of doghouse on the bit of table-land, gleaning something less than a competence by way of his bank-lines and nets, spat copiously into the muddy tide, shut one dim eye, aimed a glance at me from the other, and replied to my query:

"Take that air path," he instructed, jerking a thumb in the direction in mind, "an' keep walkin'."

"How far is it to Lost Lake?" I asked.

"All accordin' to how you-all travels," was the careful answer. "Effen you goes hoss or muleback, hit's a right smart ways. Effen you drive h'it in a rig, hit's right smart fudder. Effen you walks, hit's one helluva distance.

Good-by. Set them shank's mares to goin', stranger, effen you-all aims to git to whar you air goin' afore sundown."

I acted on that advice, and set off up a trail that rose steadily toward the crown of a wooded hill which, I was to find, was only a sort of introduction to other and steeper hills to come.

At the end of two hours I had traveled ten speedometer miles, but only about three transit ones, the excess being accumulated in the uphill and downdale progress common to locomotion in such a country. My respect for that fisherman's judgment rose momentarily—it was, indeed, "one helluva distance." A short time later, however, I came upon the first evidence of human occupation of the wilderness I had found since leaving the river. The rickety cabin and corn-cribs of Trout, the farmer.

A few minutes after reaching Trout's, and after a deal of dickering, I resumed my way, mounted on what Mr. Trout solemnly assured me was a mule. Its body resembled a length of two-by-four, its legs were like matches—but its head was truly a thing to look at and wonder over. A gigantic clawhammer with a broom-stick for a handle about describes it. On this all but inanimate skinful of bones I resumed the journey. I say I resumed the journey, because it required more exertion on my part to get my mount over the trail than it caused the mount to carry me along—if you get what I mean. A sort of slow-motion movie.

"You-all kin leave Israel with Monkey Peters at th' foot of th' lake," Israel's owner instructed me. "He'll fetch him back, after you-all pays him six-bits, or such matter, fer doin' of it."

"Fetch is right," I thought, after I'd sampled the steed's

mettle for a mile or so. "He'll have to fetch him if Israel ever sees the old homestead again. It's a cinch he'll never be able to make the return trip under his own power."

In spite of the slowness of Israel, I made better going of it than I had before adding him to my equipment. At noon I lunched beside a cold, swift hill stream, rested for an hour, Israel and myself both being in need of it, then continued the climb toward Lost Lake.

The hills were a tangle of trees of every sort, choked with undergrowth and littered with the decaying logs of centuries. The trees simply grew up, attained full maturity, then toppled to their doom. The ruggedness of the country made logging it an impossibility, so it remained just what nature, plus the destruction of the passing years, had made it.

Furthermore, I thought, it was doomed ever to remain a waste; majestic, beautiful, almost awe-inspiring, but a waste nevertheless. For the maddest industrial dreamer who ever butted his head against seeming impossibilities would have balked at thought of building a railroad there. It simply could not have been done. Without a railroad, nothing could develop that wilderness.

Lost Lake would remain lost, that appeared certain.

Presently—around the hour of two in the afternoon, I think—I entered a cañon-like passage between towering ridges clothed with small-growth post-oak and black-jack timber, buck-brush and laurel, and Israel picked his way slowly along the dry bed of what had been a creek of considerable width and depth.

I had not, since leaving civilization, given a moment's thought to the tangle I was going into the Lost Lake region to unravel, for the simple reason that it required all my wits to help the mule negotiate the trail. I remember that upon entering the cañon, I had a sense of weariness not usual with me, and an almost overpowering desire to nod—cat-nap, in fine.

Then, from out of the drowsy peace of the moment, fire rained down upon my head, streaked across it, and night came with unnatural suddenness. Total night.

I do not remember the jolt I must have received when I tumbled from Israel's back and plunged face down upon the rocks of the creek-bed, but I had evidence in plenty that it had been hard, when the darkness passed. I sat up, rubbed my eyes and looked around. The mule was nowhere to be seen, nor could my eyes detect the slightest sign of life in the cañon—unless the fat, black buzzard which sat on a limb of a dead white-oak, cocking an inquisitive eye toward my prone body, is counted.

"Not yet, old fellow!" I muttered jeeringly to the buzzard, while I sought to collect my scattered senses and halt the mad course of my head, which was outwhirling any dervish that ever dervished, or whatever it is they do. I was sick—nauseated—and, frankly, humiliated.

For, in trying to steady my head on my shoulders, I had reached a hand up shakily and discovered that my hair had been parted in an unaccustomed place. In the middle, to be exact. Parted, I will add, with a lead comb. A bullet.

3

IN NEED OF A CRUTCH

I HAD BEEN creased by a bullet which, I have no doubt, had been meant to plug me an inch or so lower down, in which case the fat buzzard would have had his meal. As it was, the ill-featured bird presently flapped reluctantly away into the timber.

Sitting there on the ground, I tried to figure out just what had happened. I knew, of course, that somebody had taken a pot-shot at me from the cover of the sloping wall of the cañon. But why? Who besides the Vans and my own office force knew that I was on my way to Lost Lake? Nobody, certainly. Yet I had been shot from ambush—and that was not all.

I made the discovery, a few minutes after my head quit whirling, that my pockets had been plundered, and that I was stripped of everything—even my guns!

"Kind of puzzled, ain't you?"

The voice was drawly, and the tone spitefully humorous. I glanced up and focused my eyes on a square-built man with a face full of black whiskers which almost obscured his mean, snakelike eyes. He sat at ease on a log not more than a dozen paces away, and the long barrel of his rifle, lying across his knees, presented its yawning muzzle directly toward me.

"Not now," I replied. "Things are getting clearer every minute. Senses coming back. For instance, I'm quite certain I heard a rattlesnake buzzing just a minute ago."

The man on the log squinted hard at me for a moment, then got up.

"Git onto them laigs, feller!" he ordered.

"What became of the legs that brought me here?" I demanded. "If harm has come to Israel—"

A loud guffaw interrupted me, and I was surprised to see the bewhiskered individual almost double up with mirth.

"Ha-ha-ha-ha-ha! Ho-ho-ho-ho-ho!" he gurgled. "Effen I hadn't seed it with my own eyes, I'd never a believed that air animile could 'a' done it! Run? Say, that relick of Noay's Ark headed eroun', soon as you-all dismounted from him lak you done, histed that rat-tail of hissen, an' was gone outa sight down th' back trail faster than airy deer I ever seed could of made it! Run! Th' dang varmint jist riz an' flew!"

"The poor devil probably caught sight of you peering over the top of a clump of brush," I commented. "No wonder he made time away from here. What in hell do you mean, lurking around that way, scaring the daylights out of honest jackasses—"

"Shet yore trap!" snarled my captor. "Ernother word lak them outten you, an' I'll let drive with this here rifle-gun, an' leave you fur th' buzzards an' wolves to pick, spite of whut th' cap'n wants done with you! Jest ernother insultin' remark, an' I'll sprinkle you all over with lead, an' don't fergit it!"

I wouldn't. He might be bluffing and he might not. So I tried a different tack.

"Thought you'd know I was joking," I complained. "To tell the truth, I can't figure out what happened to me, or whether you are a friend or a foe. Furthermore, my legs seem to have the willy-woggles; one of 'em, at least, hurts like the devil. Don't seem able to bear my weight. I'd thank you to come over here and give me a lift."

"I will—lak hell!" was the prompt retort "You jist as well not bother yoreself tryin' to think up ways to git away frum me. It kain't be did, an' that's flat. Git up on them laigs, an' lemme see how fast you kin do it!"

The rifle came up, and the lid of one of the whiskered man's eyes drooped down, the other orb sighted menacingly down the polished barrel.

Would he shoot? I asked myself the question, because the answer was important. If my mind found a positively affirmative answer, then the plot hatching in my dome would have to go into the discard. If the conviction was strong that he was not so ready to sling lead as his words proclaimed, then there was a slight chance that I would be able to turn the tables on him.

The cap'n!

Memory flashed back to what I inferred was a reference on the native's part to some one under whose orders he was acting. In all probability it was this cap'n who had creased me and robbed me. The native was, very likely, a confederate of his in some brand of deviltry concerning which I was utterly ignorant. But the mere recollection of the reference to this mysterious person helped me to my answer.

" '—spite of whut th' cap'n wants done with you!' "

That argued that the cap'n had given explicit directions concerning the disposition to be made of me—and I didn't believe the whiskered party would run counter to those instructions. Not unless he had to do so in self-defense.

I went ahead with my scheme on that hypothesis.

After two abortive efforts to stand on my feet, I dropped down and lay on the ground, moaning, and rubbing my right leg. My face, I am sure; must have touched a less stony heart than beat in the bosom of my captor. It pictured agony.

"Lord, man!" I groaned. "I must have broke it, or sprained it! Can't walk! Can't even stand!"

"You-all got to!" snarled the native. "Them's th' cap'n's orders! You git right up frum thar, or I'll whale hell outten you!"

He advanced toward me, rage turning his face almost as black as his beard. I struggled up, tottered, then crashed down again—a frightened, moaning heap.

My captor stopped about five feet from me, venting his disgust in a flow of profanity; primitive, unexpurgated profanity.

"If you'll try and find Israel, my mule," I begged, "I can get on him and ride wherever it is you want me to go. I'm willing to go, if I only can!"

"Ketch hell!" he shouted. "Think I've got wings? Old Scratch hisself couldn't ketch that varmint, once he got in motion, an' you-all knows it!"

"Maybe you could pack me on your back," I ventured hopefully.

"I see myself totin' yore carcass three miles into th' hills!" he said sarcastically. "I'd shorely like to do it, but I left my saddle at home. You'll ride shank's mare, or you'll stay here an' gorge them buzzards I done mentioned! Air you goin', or ain't you?"

Suddenly my face lit up with a happy idea, and I almost smiled at him. "I've got it!" I exclaimed. "You carry a sheath-knife, I see. Cut me a small sapling, one with a stout fork in it, and maybe I can hobble along on it as a crutch! There's one over there," I pointed out. "Get it, and I'll do my best."

The native gave me a long searching look; then, without taking his mean eyes off me for an instant, he backed away to where the sapling was growing, rifle at ready. All during the time he hacked at that sapling, his attention was riveted on me. After that job was done, he trimmed the staff according to my directions, leaving a fork at the tapered end, then tossed it on the ground where I could reach it.

But my troubles were not over. I found I couldn't raise myself, even with the assistance of the crutch.

"Once I am up, and this fork is under my right arm," I told him plaintively, "I can make it. Won't you please help me that far?"

"Damn sich as you!" the native snapped, and the next moment he had seized me roughly and was dragging me to my feet. "Now don't waste no more of my time!" he snarled.

The fork was almost under my arm, but it slipped, and I sagged down, a moan of pain forcing itself from between my agony-drawn lips.

The native leaped toward me, reached out a supporting hand—and the next instant the heavy staff, wielded with all the power of my arms and body, stretched him on the ground.

I caught up my victim's rifle, plucked a revolver from his belt, and made tracks up the cañon, taking advantage of all the cover the place afforded.

A moving shadow fell on the ground, and I glanced up. The fat buzzard, or his brother, was returning—bringing others. Funny, isn't it, how quickly those air-ghouls find their prey?"

4

MR. MONKEY PETERS

SHORTLY BEFORE DUSK I topped the crown of the highest ridge I had yet encountered, and looked down upon Lost Lake—a long body of placid water, with neither beginning nor end so far as I could see. In the gathering gloom it looked like a mile-wide strip of freshly turned black earth, furrowed by the gentlest of winds. From where I stood the ridge sloped gradually to a level strip of beach bordering the water. Across the valley rose the interminable hills; majestic, hazy, forbidding.

I made slow progress down to the beach, my head sore and achy. When I stood beside the lake I realized that insofar as discovering traces of human beings was concerned I had got nowhere. Trout had said I might leave Israel with Monkey Peters at the foot of the lake, and, while it was out of my hands to leave the animal anywhere, he having disposed of himself to my relief, I did want to get in touch with the gentleman with the simian monicker. I struck out southward.

I had not gone more than half a mile when a light suddenly sprang into life out of the bosom of the lake, its tiny flicker reflected in a long, thin streak in the water, broken by the lazy waves. It came from a quarter near what

I soon determined was the southern end of Lost Lake, and was stationary at a point about midway of it.

"Somebody's got a boat anchored out there," I surmised. "Maybe it's the monkey party."

I decided against calling out and making my presence known, and continued down the beach, eyes alert for sign of human beings. Half a quarter farther on I came upon a squat shanty of logs, and Monkey Peters.

I knew Monkey when I saw him. He looked the part, being the most-ill-assorted piece of human construction I have ever visioned. Short, thick legs, arms like long flails, insignificant body, and the hairiest hide I had ever seen off a bear or buffalo. He had the low brow, deep-set eyes and ponderous lower features of a gorilla, and when he ambled toward me I could almost believe that one such animal was truly approaching.

"Come in, set down an' rest yore feet!" he cried cordially. "Reckon you air a hunter which done got lost? Ain't many sich comes here, but all them as does gits lost, shore as you're bawn. But don't you-all worry, fur effen you war lost you air now found. Supper's done over, but th' ole wumman'll git together a snack fur you."

"Thank you, Mr. Peters," I replied. "But I want to cross the lake, if you'll show me how that may be done, as I have business at Rockaway Place."

He gave me a long, appraising look, then chuckled. "Mr. Peters!" he mimicked. "Name's Alonzo, but ever'body but me have done forgot it. Ever'body, friend and foe alike, calls me Monkey—though why they does I'm etarnally damned effen I kin figger out!"

That was said in such evident earnestness, I did not fail

to assure him that I was equally puzzled about why such a name should be applied to him. He liked my position in the matter, and grinned a broad, fang-exposing grin.

"Mought be, now; you-all would lak to stay all night with me, an' cross over til' lake in th' mawnin'?" he hazarded, honest-eyed hospitality peering out of a hairy ambush.

"Must get over to-night," I insisted. "Though I thank—"

I broke off and my glance dropped to my hands, following the lead of the native who had fixed his eyes upon them. His face, beaming good-naturedly so shortly before, had become absolutely blank.

"Fur a city feller," he commented in a slow drawl, "you-all air carryin' th' curiousist rifle-gun I ever seed one carry. Mought be, now, you-all done borried it from somebody hereabouts?"

For the first time I gave attention to the kind of gun in my hands—the property of my crutch-cutting acquaintance then furnishing the festive-board of the fat birds with which he had threatened me. It was an antiquated but sufficiently deadly model; though certainly not such an arm as a city sport would be likely to fancy. While I considered the gun, Monkey Peters continued his speculative remarks:

"Mought be you-all been stopping with Black Pete Barzen?" he offered. "Mought be huntin' in th' neighborhood of his cabin, back to'ard th' big river. I calkerlates you air. Air you?"

"Never heard of the man," I replied. "This gun belonged to my grandfather, and I cherish it because of my great affection for him. He shot Yankees with it during the Civil War, and that fact also endrars it to me. Do you want the job of rowing me across—for a silver dollar—or don't you?"

After another long look at the Yankee-killer in my hands, the native finally detached his eyes from it and himself from the subject.

"Shore I wants to earn that dollar!" he declared, and straightway led the way to where his skiff was anchored. Git in th' bow," he instructed, "an' I'll have you-all on t'other side in a jiffy."

I got in, but I faced Mr. Peters in the stern—and the heirloom of my departed grandfather faced him also.

"What's that light down at the foot of the lake?" I queried when We were half across.

"That air is whar Friendly Joe's cabinboat is anchored now," he explained.

"Friendly Joe?" I repeated questioningly. "Sounds like a right fine name, but I don't know any more now than I did before."

"Does you-all jest nacherrally hafta know about things hereabouts?" came the surprising counter.

I gave him a hard look which I fear was lost in the gloom before it reached him. "Anything I want to know," I assured him, "I'll damn well find out. Why don't you want to tell me about Friend—"

"Oh, mister, I ain't got no objections to tellin' you-all!" Peters exclaimed. "I war jest a jokin' of you! Trouble is, I kain't tell you nothin' about him, 'cept that he's been here longer than I kin remember, livin' in a cabin-boat he done built hisself, an' anchorin' it fust in one place an' then in ernother. He moves about over th' whole lake, an' it's ten mile long, whenever it pleases him to. Here lately, though, he's stuck purty clost to th' foot of Lost. That's all I knows, only that he's th' cantankeroustest old devil in th' whole world, an' th' hatein'est!"

"So," I continued, "that's why they call him 'Friendly' Joe!"

"Adzackly!"

Conversation ceased with the grounding of the skiff on a pebbly beach which was barely distinguishable in the near-night gloom. I had been wondering, all the while about the lack of life on the eastern shore of Lost, or rather the lack of evidence of life. All was dark. But when I stood on the narrow shingle and looked up through a break in the hill-wall, I saw the misty outlines of a massive building not more than a hundred yards away.

"Yander's Rock'way Place," came the voice of the boat-man. "They ain't showin' no lights they don't hafta show, here lately. Mebbe they'll tell you-all th' why of that, if you axes 'em—an' you will, in co'se, because you air th' axin' kind!"

A grating of wood on gravel, a swish of paddle-torn water, and Monkey Peters was away. I almost wished I had reserved payment of the dollar until I chose to dismiss him, but the wish was a bit tardy. He had examined the coin closely in the light of a match, before I got near enough to the shore to disembark, and then carefully pouched it in a greasy tobacco bag.

A narrow path led steeply up toward the house, and I followed it.

5

AT ROCKAWAY PLACE

SO IT WAS Black Pete Barzen's rifle I carried? Who was Black Pete, I wondered, as I negotiated the steep climb in as much silence as possible. Monkey Peters had recognized the gun, that was certain. Trust a native to know by sight the weapon of each and every inhabitant of the territory.

Well, what of it? Black Pete would never need it again, and I might as well have it. Its possession, now that it had been identified with Pete, might well lead to the identification of the mysterious "Cap'n."

In all truth, the cap'n was the party I longed to meet.

I had not tried to fathom the mystery of the, to me, unwarranted attack in the cañon. Doubtless I would find that it was in some manner connected with the business which brought me into the hinterland. Maybe not—but probably so. Time would develop the truth or falsity of that matter.

Standing on a broad, level, grass-covered plateau, I viewed the stone pile that was Rockaway Place, looking squarely into its face, so to speak. I failed to detect light at any of the windows, but that was no indication of vacancy; the blinds might well be tightly drawn.

Deciding to scout about a bit before walking up to the

big entrance, I circled toward the rear. Still no lights. No dogs, either, I considered the absence of dogs as a rather queer circumstance; a big place in the wilds, without a considerable canine establishment, didn't fit in with my knowledge of such places. At the moment, however, I welcomed their absence.

Finally, at the southwest corner of the building, I was encouraged by a narrow ribbon of light which showed beneath the lowered shade of what I took to be the establishment's morning room. I crept under the window, treading softly, and gained a view of the interior.

On a lounge at my right sat two persons; a young man of about twenty, and a girl—beautiful, let me state right here— was beside him. Her age would be about eighteen, I judged. Both were listening attentively to the remarks of a third individual, their eyes directed steadily upon him.

The third individual occupied a chair near the center of the room, and within easy view from the window. A well proportioned man of thirty-five, or thereabouts, with dead-black hair and gray eyes which looked a bit blue in the artificial light. His clean-shaved face was at the moment pleasingly animated, a smile playing—snakelike, I thought—about his thin-lipped, wide mouth. In dress he suggested a man more accustomed to cities than his present surroundings.

"—as soon as I could get away," he was finishing a remark begun before my arrival, accompanying the words with an ingratiating smile.

"We were sure you would!" exclaimed the girl.

"Without doubt, Miss Van," the black-haired party assured her. "I could not rest easy, after your letter came, until I was on the ground and prepared to do battle against your enemies! That's the sort of man Tug Norton is, and so he shall always be!"

Why—why, damn his crust!

" 'That's the sort of man Tug Norton is, and so he shall always be!'" I repeated the words again in my mind.

Bang! The theretofore mysterious incidents of the day connected themselves promptly in a clearly defined, unbreakable chain! I was now privy to the sequel of that scene in the cañon, and my aching head no longer need wrestle with a conundrum!

"Tug Norton, eh!" I gritted, madder than I remember ever to have been before, yet owning even then to a sort of admiration for such a display of superb gall. "Glad to meet you, Mr. Norton—but I'm damned if you'll be to meet me!"

There was a faint shuffle behind me, and before I finished the prompt turn I started, something hard was boring into the small of my back, and a low voice called:

"Des move one uv yo' lil fingahs, en' I blows a hole clean thoo yo'!"

It was a bad time for the party behind me to choose to stick me up, for I was mad clear through, and consequently reckless. Leaping aside, I pivoted and swung—swung hard against the point of an ebony jaw, and the possessor thereof hit the ground.

A brief glimpse verified my conviction that the man I had hit, and knocked senseless, was a negro. Then, with his revolver in hand, I made for a side entrance, the one through which he must have come when stealing up on me; the door was open a slight bit.

There had been mention of a negro servant called

Tango, in the letter from Van, and I was not at all glad of the encounter with him. Doubtless he was acting for the protection of his "white folks." However, he would not have listened to any argument of mine in regard to my identity, and I had no time to fool with him. Loss of time might prevent me from enjoying the picture of meeting myself in the room I had just been spying upon—and I'd have gone a longer ways, rather than miss it.

A short corridor led from the side entrance and joined the main one of the wing. No light showed in all that dark pile, except a faint thread which came from under the door of the room at the southwest corner. I stole to the door, my progress muffled in the springy softness of a thick carpet.

"Now," the Tug Norton in the room was saying, his voice carrying plainly to the Tug Norton in the hall, "I shall take all such precautions myself, and there is no need to disturb yourselves in the matter. Four trusted men from the Kansas City office will arrive in the morning, and they are sufficient guard for the place—and your safety. Please go about your affairs without fear. I assure you you shall be safe."

"Oh, I'm so glad you came, Mr. Norton!" cried the girl. "It has been terrible! Now we shall know something approaching relief!"

"Absolutely!" came my impersonator's voice heartily. "Relief is right! After tonight you need have no fear, because, as I said, my men will be in from the Kansas City office—"

I couldn't stand it another minute. With a sudden twist of the knob and swing of the door, I was inside, the door was closed, and my back was against it.

Miss Van cowered against the back of the lounge, her

face white and her slim body convulsed with fright. George leaped to his feet, eyes blazing and fists clenched. The effect upon the poser in the chair was instantaneous. He got up, only half smothering the profane ejaculation which had formed in his mind, and demanded:

"Who are you?"

"I'm one of the men from the Kansas City office," I replied, mimicking his tones. "One you were *not* expecting! Put your paws as high as you can get 'em—damned quick!"

Did he?

Yes, for the muzzle of Black Pete Barzen's antiquated but deadly rifle was yawning just under his nose.

6

A RETRIEVED IDENTITY

"CONTAIN YOURSELF, GEORGE," I called out in caution to young Van, who seemed on the verge of launching something troublesome. "You've just been rescued, and don't know it. Stay right where you are, and presently I'll let you in the know of it."

I prodded my imitator over against the wall near the window through which I had first observed him, and drew the blind securely. I had no wish to be a target for the Ethiop, should he recover his senses and procure another gun.

Then I shook "Mr. Norton" down—and got two excellent six-guns off him. I know they were excellent because they happened to be my own.

"Didn't keep 'em long enough to use 'em, did you, bo?" I jeered, poking him toward a chair with the rifle barrel. "Took 'em away, there in the cañon, and—"

"Mr. Van!" snapped the captive. "I demand that you end this thing, here and now! If this person is connected with you, advise him that he is in error, and that I am the detective for whom you wrote—Tug Nor—"

"Shut up!" I snarled. "Repeat that lie, and I'll not answer for the consequences—"

No words of his interrupted my remark. It was the startled look of horror in his eyes that did it. Blackhead was gazing at the rifle I held, as though the thing fascinated him.

"So you recognize it too, eh?" I said. "Last time you saw it, Black Pete was using it to insure peaceful obedience on my part. Doubtless you would like to know what became of Pete?" I paused, chuckled, then went on: "Ask the buzzards," I told him. "They know. Pete is at this moment, no doubt, inculcating all buzzardom with indigestion, and I'm the innocent cause."

"I don't know the person you call Black Pete—"

"Shut up, again!" I ordered. "When I've proved you to be the fraud you are, to the complete satisfaction of George and Rita, Ill spare you about two minutes in which to say your say—sing your swan song, as it were."

"You can't begin explaining matters a moment too soon!" declared George Van. "Who are you?"

"I'm the man this bird claimed to be," I answered. "Tug Norton, of the Kaw Valley Detective Bureau, Kansas City—at your service. This chap and a native named Black Pete Bazren, whose rifle gun I am now carrying, waylaid me in a cañon west of the lake this afternoon, downed me with a rifle bullet, and plundered my person. My shield, guns, papers, all were taken—enabling this fellow to impersonate me. How I got away from Black Pete need not occupy our time now, nor is it essential that we try to determine how the news that you had sent for me leaked out. It did leak out, as we have just had proved to us. It is, however, very important that the matter of identities be settled at once, here and now."

"Don't listen to the lies this fellow is telling!" exclaimed Blackhead. "I'm just who I claim to be! Didn't I show you my credentials—even the letter you wrote to me? Now this scoundrel comes along and cooks up a yarn about getting shot, losing his papers, and all that rot—"

"He did have your letter, George!" Rita broke in. "That would seem to prove—"

"Nothing at all!" George interrupted. "This new Tug Norton looks like he might have been in a mighty tight place recently. There's blood—"

"Yeah!" I cut in in my turn. "And here's the further evidence!"

I bared my head and bent over so the long, red parting in the middle of my hair could be plainly seen.

"Oh! Oh!" gasped Miss Van. "You have been hurt! Your head has bled terribly!"

"Sound as a new dollar!" I assured her—"But thanks for your sympathy. Now," I went on, "as to this bird in the chair. Say, what's the manufacturer's number on your shield? On the back? Quick, answer up!"

The crook drew himself up dignifiedly. "I'm not going to cheapen myself by attempting to prove a thing which should be unquestioned by those I have sought to serve," he said severely.

"You'll be cheaper'n that, old timer," I notified him, "if you don't loosen up and talk when told to. Don't let my gay and festive manner mislead you, for it is only seeming. You never was nearer becoming a cheap article in your life than you now are. A free feed for the buzzards, like your black pal, to be definite. Goin' to talk?"

"Why don't you speak up in your own defense?" George demanded, approaching the counterfeit presentment and looking at him out of eyes which were beginning to glow with anger. "Why sit there like a dolt, and refuse to talk."

"The man has asked a question I cannot answer properly," was the reply. "I have never noticed the number on the back of my shield, although I am aware that one is there—"

"Liar!" I broke in. "There is no number on the reverse of the shield! Take if off him, George," I ordered, "and look for yourself!"

Van, with the aid of my long-barreled persuader, possessed himself of the shield, looked at it while Rita peered interestedly over his shoulder, and then threw it on a table with a snort of disgust.

"No number at all!" he declared. "But you haven't proved yourself, merely by what may have been a trick of memory on your part—"

"All in good time, my dear George," I soothed. "I'm going to prove up clean before I stop. Say, you," I demanded, again facing the man in the chair, "did you write a letter advising these young folks that you would arrive to-day?"

"Certainly."

"We got the letter," Rita seconded, Paul Lemaitre, our boatman, brought it in from Kirkland last evening."

"Fine!" I applauded. "Now, Mister Whatsyourname, can you repeat, verbatim, the contents of that letter?"

It was a poser, and I knew it. Did Blackhead flop? He did not.

"I do not concern myself with the actual composition of letters to my clients," he stated pompously. "My secretary wrote that I would arrive to-day—and I did so arrive."

I laughed. Had to. Blackhead's performance was becoming ludicrous. Then I repeated, word for word, the brief letter I had dictated to my stenographer.

Miss Van clapped her hands softly, in applause. "He did it!" she cried. "That is just what was in the letter!"

"I believe you are right, Rita," George agreed.

"Have you the letter handy?" I inquired.

Rita ran to a secretary, opened a drawer and took up a folded sheet of paper. "Here it is!" she cried, eyes shining.

"Don't open it," I bade her. "Lay it on the table—there, keep the writing concealed." I took a fountain pen from my pocket and wrote my name on the blank side. "Compare the inks and the signatures—"

Blackhead, seeing me occupied at the table, thought the opportunity to depart too good to pass up. He rose and dashed for the door, flung it open just as I drew a bead on his left thigh with the intention of dropping him—then staggered back into the room, an oath on his lips.

In the aperture occasioned by the opened door, stood a tall, ebony-black negro, and his right hand steadily gripped a gun.

"The signatures are identical!" I seemed to hear Rita shout as from a distance. "Ink is the same, too!"

"Ah wants me some explunations!" stated the black with the gun. "Somebody done hit me on de jawbone, an' dey ain't neider uv you two white gemmen goin' to leave dis house ontwel I fin's out which 'un done did it!"

"Sit down, Blackhead!" I called with all the sarcasm I could muster. "You are covered front and rear—sit down!"

He sat—or rather, sank—down in a chair as ordered.

The huge black stalked slowly into the room, the whites of his eyes shot with red anger.

7

INSIDE STONE WALLS

"TANGO!"

It was Miss Van who spoke. Her voice was stern, and the negro turned his eyes upon her as she walked across the room toward him.

"Missie, somebody done hit—"

"Put the revolver in your pocket!" the girl commanded, coming to a stop before the black and eying him sternly. "Put it away, and stand over by the door. When you are wanted, you will be told."

Tango's face, hard as pig iron before, softened under the influence of the young woman's gaze, and, pocketing the pistol, he returned to the door and stationed himself beside it—a servant once more.

I turned in explanation to Miss Van. "Tango shoved a gun against my spine," I told her, "while I was peering into this room through the window, I couldn't spare the time to argue with him just then, so I was compelled to knock him down. Sorry, but it had to be."

Miss Van smiled. "I understand," she assured me.

I approached the black, fumbling in my bill fold which I had recovered from Blackhead. "I have here a sort of plaster, famously soothing for aching jawbones," I told him. "Try it." I slipped a twenty-dollar bill into his willing hand.

"White folks is sho' funny," he philosophized aloud a moment later, showing all his teeth in a grin. "Ruthah knock a niggah down, an' pay foh it, den argy wid him!"

Blackhead, no longer maintaining even a pretense of his former attitude, sat slumped in his chair, brow heavy, and smoldering eyes fixed on me.

"George," I asked, "does this château boast something in the way of a dungeon—say a cellar room, dark, damp, and full of rats? It must have, in addition to the rodents, windowless walls and a door that is escape proof. Have you any such built-in convenience as that?"

"There's the ex-wine cellar," George replied with a grin. "It's sure to fill the bill."

"Have you a stout chain and a pair of padlocks on the premises?"

"Tango will get them," he answered, and motioned the negro out of the room.

"All right." I sat down and fixed my eyes on those of the disgruntled crook. "When those four men you spoke of arrive from Kansas City," I told him, "you will have company to help while away the dark tedium of your confinement. If you were lying about them, you may now begin to contemplate the lonely hours in store for you. I rather think you have arranged for a few accomplices to show up here in the guise of honest sleuths, but whether they do or not is of very little moment.

"Now get this straight," I went on. "You are being given a chance to talk things over with me—come through, I mean. You will or you won't, of course—but, bear this in mind: you will get only the one chance. Once you are in the wine cellar, there you will stay until you leave it for the county bastile, and, later, the gallows. Going to talk, and get a little hide-insurance for yourself while the getting is good?"

"You haven't got anything on me," Blackhead gritted, "and you can't frame me. I know nothing of what you are talking about. I'm a duly licensed detective, and I can prove it. Now crack your whip!"

"I'll crack your nerve instead," I answered easily. "You'll talk, and gladly, before I'm through with you. In the meantime," I continued, as the door opened to admit the negro, "we'll visit the wine cellar. I see Tango is ready for us."

It required the combined strength of the negro and myself to get our captive down the stairs into the big cellar, but we finally managed it. In a dark corner of the place, lit by a lantern in the hands of George, we stopped before a stout door of heavy oak timbers, complemented with a lock-and-chain arrangement which would have defied the skill of Houdini. Tango opened the door, and we deposited our burden on the damp, rock floor of the cellar.

Miss Van joined us, carrying a thick blanket. "It will be very cold down here," she said to me. "And, after all, he is a human being."

"Rather than contradict you," I returned, "I'll allow that he is, and permit him the soft luxury you offer. He don't deserve it, and may thank you for it. Personally, I'd rather bed him down on a cake of ice."

" 'The kind of man Tug Norton is, and so he shall always be!' "

That speech was still rankling, you may be sure. He was lucky to get the blanket.

In the center of the cellar stood a thick shoring-post, and to that I chained Blackhead securely. One loop of the chain was passed about his middle, the links secured with a lock—and there wasn't any slack in the loop. He'd stay there, so far as his unaided efforts to escape were concerned.

Holding the lantern high, I surveyed the place minutely. The room was below the ground level, getting its meager ventilation through slits in the partition which separated it from the main cellar, and the walls were good heavy rocks, set by masons who knew their job.

"Ever hear that mush about 'stone walls do not a prison make,' old timer?" I jibed, as I was in the act of closing Blackhead in with the rats. "The bird that made that wise crack would have rated high alongside of Ananias. If you take issue with me," I grinned, pointing to the walls that guarded him, "have at 'em!"

8

STUBBORN KNOTS

AN APPETIZING SUPPER, of which I stood greatly in need, was served me in the handsome dining room directly we finished with the prisoner. A stony-faced woman, French by the look of her, attended. While I ate, I probed into things.

"In the first place," I asked, "can you give me an inkling of what all this rumpus is about?"

George Van shook his head in a vigorous negative. "Beyond the fact that my father was shot down by a person unknown, and that two attempts have been made to commit further murder, I know nothing."

"Well, there is something," I assured him. "Something in the nature of a powerful motive back of it all. Men do not go about killing folks for no cause at all. Whoever killed your father had an end to serve—an end which urged him to shed blood, and which he put before everything else in the world, his own neck included.

"But subsequent events have proved that the end in view was not consummated in the death of one member of your family. Had those attempts on your life and that of Miss Van not been made, I would lean to the theory entertained by the coroner—that of accidental shooting. Some men are so constituted as to render them unable to come forward and acknowledge to an accident of that nature, though why they should fear to do so I confess I can't fathom. Fear to own the deed would account for the non-appearance of an accidental killer, if one existed.

"There is, too, another possibility," I went on. "Revenge for some real or fancied wrong. Even under the circumstance we are dealing with, I can imagine a revenge-driven maniac whose lust demands the extinction of your entire family. Such cases have occurred. Perhaps a painstaking review of Roger Van's past will give us a clew."

I paused for comment. George answered promptly.

"If father had incurred the enmity of such a person," he said, "he never mentioned the matter in my hearing. The only period of his past which might have produced the revenge-driven maniac you mentioned dates back about fifteen years. I will explain.

"Rita and I are children of father's first wife. She died when we were very young—six and four, respectively. A few years later father married again; a handsome woman who was much younger than he. The union was unfortunate, its end tragic. A full account of the matter may be found on the court records in Kansas City, where we then resided.

"After father killed the man in the case, and turned his faithless wife out of his house, he retired from business and dropped out of sight. No jury, in those days, would convict a man for wiping out one who had betrayed him as father was betrayed, and he was acquitted.

"One day, a year after he disappeared, father came and removed my sister and me from the home of an aged aunt with whom he had left us, and brought us here to Lost

Lake. We lived in a log cabin while this house was being built. Father had great wealth, and he desired to purchase solitude with it. He achieved his purpose, as you have only to look around you to determine.

"If his death, and the attacks on his children, is an aftermath of that old tragedy I shall be greatly surprised. We have lived here in peace with every one since we came. Father, after a time, became the serene, gentle man he remained until the moment of his death. No one from the outside ever came here and disturbed him. I do not believe the unfortunate incident I have described had anything to do with his taking off."

"Nor do I," seconded Rita.

"Maybe not," I replied. "Who was the chap your father killed? Did he have standing in the world, or any family?"

"He was an idler of considerable wealth," George answered. "Arthur Stanhope, by name. A handsome scoundrel whose evil deeds had found him out long before his charm of manner lured my stepmother into her misstep. He had standing only among his own kind. His relatives were shocked at his end, of course, but their sympathies were wholly with father. There were two brothers in his immediate family, and both are now engaged in the practice of law in Kansas City,"

"Jeff and Dick Stanhope. Yes, I know them. Fine fellows, and may be counted out of this mess," I commented. "But the cast-out wife may not be so easily disposed of," I went on. "She may have thirsted for revenge."

"If so, she had a strange way of showing it," George declared. "She married again within less than a year. This time her union was with one of her own kind. A gambler who has since, I am informed, kept her in the style of flashy luxury she craves. St. Louis is their home. Judge for yourself whether she is a probable factor in the case."

"I think we may pass her up," I replied. "Was there a child born of this second marriage?"

"No."

"Had there been—but there wasn't," I broke off. "Pass the second wife. If she is a specimen true to her type, she's too shallow to harbor hatred or any other deep passion. What relatives have you?"

"Some cousins, distantly connected and widely scattered," George informed me. "One near relative only. You may know him, since he has a business connection in Kansas City. Frank Leverage, only brother of my mother."

"The sand man, eh? Yeah, I know him. His sand dredges are pretty prominent in the Missouri and the Kaw," I commented. "Tall, jolly chap. Something of a globetrotter-hunts big game in Europe, and all that sort of stuff."

"That's Uncle Frank, all right," George agreed with a smile. "While not immensely wealthy, he possesses income enough to enable him to humor any whim that enters his head. And they are many. He was in Europe at the time of father's death, but hurried home when advised of it."

"Did he visit Rockaway Place often during your father's lifetime?"

"He came here occasionally for the fall duck shooting, which is exceptionally good," George informed me. "Sometimes alone, and sometimes accompanied by a friend or two. Things were always merry for sister and me when Uncle Frank was here, and we always cried when he went away. I am quite sure he is fond of us, too, for he never fails to come loaded down with presents. An unusually attractive person is Uncle Frank."

"Humph! He's your nearest kin, isn't he?"

"Yes."

"He'd inherit from you in the event of your death—I mean should you and your sister die without issue?"

"We can leave our money and property to any one we choose," George pointed out.

"But have you made wills in favor of any one?" I demanded.

"No. We are both single, and should we die without issue I know of nobody whom I would prefer to have what we leave than Uncle Frank."

"Mr. Norton," Rita broke in, "if you are thinking that Uncle Frank might be at the bottom of all this trouble, please dismiss that thought. He is not at all that kind. Besides, he has all the money he needs. He has our love and confidence."

"Young lady," I pointed out, "in this game of sleuthing it is necessary to examine all the possibilities, and not merely those which seem likely to bear fruit. I'd pick you to pieces, as well as George, if I were examining into the murder of your father, instead of what I am doing. I'm not accusing Frank Leverage. I'm not in position to accuse anybody— yet. We'll pass Uncle Frank, now, and go on to others. How many servants do you employ?"

"A cook, housemaid, boatman and forester—the Paul Lemaitre of whom I have already spoken—and Tango. The latter came here with father, and served as a sort of combination butler and valet to him. When we desire extra servants," Miss Van continued, "we get them at the French settlement, five miles up the lake. All those now employed, save Tango, are French."

"And there has never been any friction between your father, or yourselves, and these French people, or any one hereabouts?"

"None whatever."

"Well," I commented, arising from the supper table and lighting a cigar, "the more I examine this tangle the less I think of it. Believe me, the knots of its composition are stubborn. But once we get a lead, if only the tiniest of threads, we'll straighten it all out. What do you say to turning in for the night? Things will be safe enough for the next few hours, and I think there is no need to keep watch. After the plight of our friend Blackhead becomes known—then look out!"

Half an hour later, after Miss Van had washed and bandaged the parting in my hair, I was enjoying a very gratifying snooze.

9

AN EXPLOSION OF A SORT

NEXT MORNING I accompanied Tango when he went down to feed Blackhead. The breakfast was much better than I would have accorded him, but, detecting the fine, sympathetic hand of pretty Miss Rita in the preparation of the tray, I voiced no remonstrance.

The prisoner merely sat up on his blanket and gave us a mean look when we entered.

"Here's something the chef of the Ritz sent down to you," I told him. "You ought to be glad you're in jail, with such grub as that to bless your interior. I daresay, though, you are not appreciative. Want to talk?"

"When my turn comes—yes."

"Oh, you're expecting a turn of some kind then? Well, if yours fails to materialize, I can promise you one for a certainty. A turn of a rope around your gullet. Does the prospect allure?"

No answer—just a venomous glare.

We left him to his food, and returned to the upper floor. George and Rita were not visible, it being shortly after dawn, and after Tango had dug up a pair of fieldglasses for me I went out and took a walk along the ridge above the lake.

It was a sight to inspire one with the fire of a Shelley, that lake in the early morning. No mist lay over it, and, looking down from the heights, I noted that the water had a trick of appearing almost black. Depth, and the character of the dark rocks which littered the hills and which doubtless lay on the bottom of the lake, would account for that. Across the valley the ridges were shrouded in misty veils, with here and there a spot of sunlight glimmering on the polished surface of a bowlder.

Strolling along the ridge, I searched the vicinity with my glasses. Far to the north, toward the head of the lake, a number of boats were to be seen. Fishermen about their daily tasks, I surmised. I found Monkey Peters, smoking in front of his cabin door, taking his ease on the step. Then I swung my glasses toward the foot of the lake, and picked up Friendly Joe's cabin-boat.

It lay at anchor about a mile distant—a queer-looking craft which appeared to have been constructed of odds and ends of boards and saplings, though what sort of a hull it had I could not determine. I'd give Joe the once over later.

I had reached a point about half a mile below the house, when my attention was attracted to the queer appearance of the rocks which lay about me. From mottled they had become dead black, and when I examined them closely, I got a jolt.

"Coal!" I exclaimed. "Great lumps of coal! Well, I'll be damned!"

I started at a trot for the house, and came upon George Van on the bluff just below it.

"Hey, George!" I called sharply. "Why the devil didn't

you mention the fact that this section has about all the coal that hasn't already been mined, in Missouri?"

George advanced to where I stood, took the chunk of coal I held in my hand, looked at it scornfully and tossed it into the lake.

"Why mention so unimportant a matter as that?" he asked.

"Unimportant!" I exclaimed. "Why, man, there's thousands of tons in sight—just lying there for somebody to pick up! Rich? Why—"

"No, Mr. Norton, you are wrong," George corrected. "Not rich—save in its quality. There is certainly a tremendous lot of coal showing, and engineers say that the earth hereabouts is full of it—but it isn't worth anything. Suppose, now, you had to mine this coal and transport it to market at a profit? You saw a sample of the sort of country by which we are surrounded, when you came in yesterday. It is the same, maybe worse, in all other directions. Do you feel thrilled now?"

I didn't. My coal mine had exploded. Those black, oily chunks were about as valuable as are rocks in the Rocky Mountains. I saw it, then.

"Your pardon, George," I begged. "And you may kick me if you wish. I'm a dolt. A railroad into this region is the only thing that could confer value upon the coal—and that will never come. Couldn't, in fact. Even if one could be built, which I doubt, it would cost more to construct it than the coal would be worth. So—here I dismiss what at first looked like a clew!"

George laughed. "If I could sell our land as a coal field," he said humorously, "I'd be as rich as the richest manufacturer of four-cylinder motor cars. But nobody would want it. As you say, nothing short of a miracle could give this section a railroad."

"How much of this do you own, George?" I queried.

"All you can see from this spot," he replied. "And a lot more that you can't. We own the lower two miles of the lake, and far into the hills on the other side. On this side, there are two thousand acres, lying in a body along the lake shore and extending below it and far to the east, which are included in the estate. Father bought lavishly—at about three dollars per acre. He wanted to exclude everybody but ourselves from this shore of Lost—and he did. Monkey Peters is on our ground, and old Joe is anchored in 'our' lake," he grinned. "We could legally exclude them, but there is no reason for doing so."

"About Monkey Peters," I queried, "what sort of a fellow is he?"

"A lot handsomer inside than out." George replied. "Monkey is lazy, improvident, but a good soul for all that."

"And Friendly Joe?"

"Nobody knows anything about Joe," he answered. "At least nobody does who will tell—if there really is anything to tell. Some of the older settlers in the French colony, up the lake, could give up some facts about him, I think, but they won't."

"That's something else I'm curious about," I told him. "How came a settlement of French folks to be here?"

"Simple in the explanation." George replied. "Their history is wrapped up in the history of Lost Lake. I'll tell you about them and it."

10

HOW LOST LAKE WAS LOST

WE SAT DOWN on a bowlder overlooking the water, and George gave me the story:

"Missouri was largely settled, as you must know, by Frenchmen and women," he began. "They were scattered in groups along the main water courses, particularly the Mississippi and the Missouri. A colony of them came here and settled, sixty-odd years ago—"

"But this isn't a river," I interrupted. "This is, strictly speaking, nowhere at all!"

"When they came here," George said patiently, "they established their village on the east shore of the Missouri River—for Lost Lake was once a part of the river.

"You are, or should be, aware that the Missouri is the most obstinate and whimsical of streams, not even excepting the Mississippi. It changes its course when it will, and lays a new one where it listeth. Some time after the settlement was established, an earthquake occurred in this vicinity which changed the whole face of it. Hills were created where none existed before, and valleys and lowlands appeared where hills had been. After the quake was over, it was found that the Missouri had left this section and made for itself a channel far to the west. Lost Lake alone remained as a reminder of its one-time course.

"Even the lake would have disappeared, were it not for two circumstances which I shall point out. It is cut off at the southern end by a natural barrier which the quake threw up, and is replenished by the flow of hundreds of springs in the hills. Sometimes the water rises in the spring, creating a very attractive falls at the lower end, where the surplus spills over the natural dam and spreads into the hollow below.

"The French settlement was all but destroyed by the cataclysm, but its founders rebuilt, and their numbers increased. They were loath to leave so fine a hunting and trapping region, to say nothing of the fishing. Twice a year they take their furs to market, and, on the whole, are a happy, contented people—losing nothing because of their isolated location. Their name for Lost is Lac le Noir—suggested by the blackish color of the water."

"Very interesting," I commented, seeing that he had finished. "Now, about Friendly Joe. Surely there are rumors afloat concerning him? There always are tales told about such a character as he. Tell me all you know of them."

"Some say that he was a skipper of a steamboat which now lies at the bottom of the lake, it having been in this stretch of the river when the quake occurred. He, the story goes, was the sole survivor, and was rescued by the settlers. The shock of the loss of his boat and all hands, it is said, affected his mind, and he thinks that some day the river will return here, or the lake will find the river, and his boat will be restored. That's one tale, and the age of the man does not contradict the possibility of its being true.

"Another yarn is very similar to the first, save in the denouement," he went on. "It runs about the same, except that its adherents assert that Joe's boat was carrying a cargo of silver bars—millions of dollars' worth, they have it—and Joe haunts the lake in an effort to locate the wreck and retrieve the silver.

"Nobody, however, doubts that Joe is mentally deficient—whether from the shock attending the loss of his boat, or from other and unspecified causes. He is gruff, quarrelsome if approached, but, I think, utterly harmless. Why don't you call on him?"

"I shall," I told him. "But there are other more important things to do at the moment. For instance, I want to have a stroll on the terrace where your father was killed, and size up the place. Another important thing is to determine, if possible, how Blackhead and his gang got wind of the fact of my coming. I think that part should prove easy to solve. Certain precautions, too, must be taken against a repetition of the tragedy on the terrace. You may be sure that as soon as it becomes known that Blackhead is a prisoner, more bullets will come our way."

"Mr. Norton," George asked, turning trouble-shadowed eyes upon me, "what, do you think, was this Blackhead's purpose in gaining admittance to Rockaway as he did?"

"Two attempts had been made on the lives of you and your sister," I replied. "Both were abortive. Blackhead meant to make sure that the third attempt would not be an attempt only. As Tug Norton, the detective for whom you had sent, he would be in your confidence. Above all, he would be in the house, where he could work at short range. Frankly, George," I assured him with all the earnestness I myself felt, "had I been killed yesterday, instead of merely wounded, you would not now be living. Neither would Rita. That, I am sure, was what Blackhead meant to do last night—kill both of you while you slept."

An ejaculation of horror broke from George's pale lips, and the next instant he was on his feet, pointing to a boat which had, during our preoccupation, come quite near the point where we were sitting.

"Paul Lemaitre!" he exclaimed. "And he seems to be in a hurry. Coming here, too. News of some kind, you may be sure, when Paul hurries!"

11

LEMAITRE REPORTS

THE BOATMAN BEACHED his bateau and came up to us with speed. A picturesque figure, he made, hesitating for a moment on top of the bluff while he apparently awaited a signal from George to come forward.

Slender, and of medium height, he had the appearance of great strength, together with the further blessing of rugged health. His black hair was worn long, almost to his shoulders, and his eyes, coal black, were large, lustrous and protruding. A flaming red shirt, tucked into trousers of dark blue material and banded with a colorful strap that was more scarf than belt, constituted his costume. He was bare, both as to head and feet.

"What is the news you bring, Paul?" George called.

"Ah, *m'sieu'!*" cried the Frenchman, hastening to us. "Ze fish'men have beeg news! Renee Lebrun, he feesh wit grab-hooks for net he lose, an' w'at you t'ink? He ketch dose hook on heavy t'ing. Damn log, Renee t'ink. Den he haul up hard on dat line, an', *m'sieu'*, eet ees iron grate he have caught on dat grab, not no log at all!"

"An iron grate? What of it? Why so much excite—"

"Ah, *m'sieu'*, but you know not w'at dat grate she been

from!" remonstrated Paul. "W'en you know, zen you not ask for why ze eexcite!"

"So? Well, then, Paul, suppose you enlighten us," George suggested.

The Frenchman swelled with importance, his eyes becoming bigger and rounder than common. "Eet ees ze grate of a boiler dat once was steamboat boiler!" he cried. "Steamboat she sink dere! Frien'ly Joe, she maybe hees boat! W'at you t'ink?"

George turned inquiring eyes in my direction, as though soliciting my opinion. I had none, really, but gave one nevertheless. A detective is expected to always have opinions on every mysterious subject under the sun, and I wanted to be in form.

"If there is any truth in the story about Joe's boat," I stated judicially, "then it may well be that a valuable find has been made. It should be borne in mind, however, that more than one boat may have gone down in these waters. That being likely, too much importance should not be accorded the grate M. Lebrun has brought up."

"Quite right!" George agreed. "It may be any one of a dozen grates now lying on the rocks of Lost Lake. Still, the matter should be investigated, don't you think?"

"Undoubtedly," I assured him. "Such a cargo as is accredited to Joe's alleged boat may be down there, though it could hardly represent a total of millions as the story has it. If that is true, then it might explain much that we are interested in finding out. It might be the key to the whole matter, in fact. Let an investigation be made, by all means."

"We drag ze bottom of Lac le Noir queek!" exclaimed the Frenchman. "We fin' money, she be all ours—eh?"

"Unless the United States Government lays claim to it, yes," I replied. "Probably a case of losers weepers, finders keepers. Go to it, and much luck."

"T'ank you, *m'sieu'!*"

"Don't mention it. Tell me, Lemaitre, who, besides yourself, saw the letter you carried out to Kirkland and mailed to Kansas City a few days ago?"

Paul gave me a startled glance, and his denial came swiftly. "Not one mans!" he exclaimed vehemently. "I show heem nobody, jus' lak M. Van she tell me not!"

"So I thought," I assured him, "but wanted to make sure. Anybody see the letter you brought back?"

"I show heem to nobody!"

"Good!" I exclaimed. "You are very trustworthy, M. Paul, and I congratulate my young friend on being served by such a man. Who, may I ask, is—or was—Black Pete Barzen? Did you know him?"

"Ah, yes, I know dat Black Pete," he acknowledged. "You know heem, too, *m'sieu'?*"

"Met him once," I answered. "Have you heard anything about him lately? See him on any one of those letter-carrying trips?"

"I not see dat Black Pete for long time," was the reply. "He not come to dis place ver' much. We not lak heem, *m'sieu'.*"

"Why not?"

"Mebbe because he not lak us," Paul replied. "We not get 'long togedder, dat Pete an' us."

"Did you know that he is dead?" I asked sharply.

The Frenchman's face depicted genuine astonishment.

"Mon Dieu! I not hear nossing 'bout dat!" he ejaculated. "W'en he die?"

"Lately," I evaded.

"But, *m'sieu',* he not dead two, t'ree days ago—"

"How do you know?" I demanded sharply. "You said you had not seen him for some time."

Paul was not in the least disturbed. "So I say, *m'sieu',*" he said politely. "Eet ees my cousin, Pierre Lemaitre, who report having see dat Black Pete in ze woods two, t'ree days ago."

"Ah," I said, a trifle disgruntled, "your cousin, eh? Well, it is not important who saw him."

"Here comes Monkey Peters," George informed me, pointing off over the lake. "Got somebody in the boat with him, and heading for our landing. No one is expected. I wonder who it can be?"

12

A VISITOR ARRIVES

"WHY—IT'S UNCLE FRANK!" George Van exclaimed a few minutes later. "Just like him to come without notifying us about it! But he's welcome—doubly so, now that we are in trouble."

"Ahoy on shore!" boomed a voice, and a big man stood up in the bow of the approaching boat, waving his hat. "Is breakfast ready?"

"Will be soon!" George called, laughing. "Are you always hungry?"

"Born that way, and never got over it!" came the answer.

George went down the path to meet his uncle, and Lemaitre disappeared in the direction of the house. Leverage was a big, red-faced man, dressed in knickerbockers, and his voice boomed like the smothered beating of a bass drum. When he stood on the plateau, hand outstretched to grip mine, I had only to imagine him clothed in a fur coat and his resemblance to a bear was complete. His fine, white teeth, displayed by his smile, carried out the resemblance.

"So you're Tug Norton!" he roared, giving my hand a hearty shake. "Kaw Valley Bureau. Heard of you, of course, but this is the first time I've had the pleasure of coming to grips with you, as it were. Well, well! I'm certainly astonished at the news George spilled as we came up from the beach. What the devil is going on here, anyhow?"

I shot George a reproving glance, but it really was not his fault that he had divulged the presence of our prisoner. I should have cautioned him. However, in all probability, no harm had been done.

"I've heard of you, too, Mr. Leverage," I assured him in turn. "And as to what is going on here, I'll confess I'm as much in the dark as you are. Seems there's a plot on foot to wipe out the Vans, root and branch, judging from what has occurred."

"Why didn't you communicate with me, George?" Leverage demanded, turning to his nephew. "Chances are, had I not decided to run down for a bit of bass fishing I'd have known nothing about it. As it is, I'm going to stay, now I'm here, until the whole thing is cleared up. Ought to be a valuable addition to the garrison, Norton," he went on, "as I can say without fear of contradiction that I'm a crack shot with a rifle—hunted game all over the world, you know. The trouble is," he added ruefully, "I didn't bring one along!"

I'll lend you one," I told him. "One I acquired yesterday. A bit old-fashioned, to be sure, but a rattling good gun for all that."

"Thanks. Now I'm going to hurry up to the house and see Rita—then breakfast. Hope you've got plenty cooked, George, for you know what I can do once my feet are under the table!"

He hurried off toward the house, and I turned to George. "Tell Monkey Peters to come up here," I requested. "I want to talk to him."

George summoned the native, who still sat in his boat, and Monkey climbed up to us.

"Peters," I said, when he stood before me, "I want you to tell me a few things which I am sure you are able to tell. In doing so you will not be merely satisfying my idle curiosity; you will be helping Mr. Van and his sister—and they will, I answer for it, see that you lose nothing by it."

"Mr. Norton is quite right, Peters," George assured him. "I shall reward you well if you are able to give us the information we seek."

Monkey scratched his beard reflectively, his eyes staring off over the lake. Finally he said:

"I ain't wishful to git in no trouble, Mr. Van. Folks as talks too much soon quits talkin' a-tall—in these here parts. Whut does you-all want to know?"

"The name of the man whom you put across the lake to this place yesterday, shortly before you rowed me across," I said slowly.

"How you-all figger I knows his name?"

"Do you?" I jingled a pair of silver dollars suggestively.

"Mought be I do."

"I'm waiting," I suggested.

"His name air Dave Barzen," Monkey replied slowly, as though reluctant to part with the information, yet unable to resist the chance of picking up some easy money. "He air a brother to Black Pete, whose rifle gun you-all war a totin' yistiddy."

Here was news—real news! I dissembled my surprise and questioned further.

"Do you know when he came to this part of the country?" I queried. "I ask because it is patent that he has not dwelled here with Pete. He is better educated than the other, and shows the polish only a city can give. What about it?"

"I reckons he got polished in th' penitenshury," Monkey Peters averred sarcastically. "Him an' Pete got sont up fur stealin' truck offen th' gove'mint boats which war rip-rappin' th' Missouri at Tiger Bend. Le's see, that's been twelve year ago. Pete served two year, then cum back. Dave served his time, too, but didn't cum back. I hadn't seed him in so long I skursely knowed him, when he showed up yistiddy. An' he never let on lak he knowed me, nuther. Mebbe he didn't—an', gents, I won't be sorry if he didn't."

"Is that all you can tell us about the Barzen brothers?" I asked.

"I don't know nothin' else, 'cept that Black Pete war as mean a varmint as ever prowled these woods, an' Dave use to be as bad. That's all."

"You've earned this ten dollar note I'm going to give you, Peters," I said, rising and extending the money. "Let me know anything else you can find out about the Barzens—Dave in particular. Where he came from when he arrived here yesterday—that bit of information would be worth about twenty dollars. Yes—fifty. Think you can find out?"

"Fifty!" the native gasped, looking at me with wide eyes, "Mister, I don't know if I kin or not—but, Godalmighty! I kin shorely try!"

"Then get at it," I suggested. "The sooner the better."

"Well," George queried, after the native had departed and we were on our way to the house, "was the information worth the money?"

"And then some!" I declared. "A brother to Black Pete

Barzen! I no longer wonder at the horror in his eyes last night when he recognized his brother's rifle in my hands! That rifle probably told him that Pete was dead, else in a lot of trouble. We've made headway, and no mistake."

"About Lebrun's find?" he asked. "Is that important to us?"

"Not a bit," I returned. "There may be a lot of silver on the bottom of the lake, but you can dismiss the thought, if you have such, that it has any connection with' your trouble. Give me about two days in which to follow a lead which came to me while I was talking with Monkey, and I'll give you a surprise that will lift you off your feet. I promise. Now," I went on, shaking my head positively in negation, as his mouth opened to pour forth questions, "lead me to that terrace, then you can go and play with Uncle Frank."

13

BLACKHEAD SPORTS A GRIN

THE LOWER TERRACE, referred to by George in his letter to me, lay on the east side of the house and was reached by a flight of stone stairs from the upper level. A well kept path led from the lower level into the hills beyond. George pointed out the location of his father's body when found, and reckoning from that it was easy to approximately fix the spot in which the assassin had stood. A search of the hillside would probably reveal the exact location, but I was not interested in that.

When I judged that breakfast would be about ready I returned to the house. At table, Leverage discussed the subject which was uppermost in all our minds, pro and con, and finally informed us of his conviction that somebody was trying to get revenge on the Vans because of some grudge against one or more of them.

"I have no idea who it could be," he said, replying to a question, "nor what could have caused the grudge. But, look at the thing from any angle, and it will jibe with nothing else. Nobody covets this place, that is certain. Besides, should any one wish to get possession of it, the obvious method would be by purchase. Certainly nobody would commit murder to acquire it. Had any offers lately, George?"

"You know of the offers father received, uncle," George reminded. "We have been approached by an agent, since he died, on behalf of the party who tried to buy before. Needless to say, we refused to discuss selling."

"Montgomery Nash, if I remember correctly, wanted the place as a summer residence," Leverage said. "Don't blame him for that, because there is no better bass lake in the State, and the spot is Old Man Mallard's back yard. Nash is able to afford anything that strikes his fancy, and doubtless raised the ante over the price he offered Roger. Did he?"

George nodded. "My refusal was final," he said. "The place is not on the market, nor will it be. Rita and I are one in that resolve."

"Nash, the live stock exchange man?" I queried. "Is he the man who wants to buy?"

"He's the man," George affirmed.

I went on with my ham-and, taking no further part in the table-talk. I was picturing in the eyes of my mind the Montgomery Nash I knew. A weazened, milk-and-water money grubber, with about as much use for a casting rod or duck gun as I have for a game of flinch, or croquet. I visioned the ancient pile of crumbling bricks he occupied as a home in Kansas City—a relic of the early sixties, in a location abandoned to cheap boarding houses—and I couldn't feature him putting out a lot of money for a palace in the hills.

If Nash had made offers for the place, then it was worth, at least to him, vastly more than any sum he named. Not that he wasn't rich enough to pay any amount at all, for that matter. The point is that he wouldn't, unless he already had a big profit on the deal in sight.

What had Nash seen in the place to make him want to take it over? Had he entertained any such notion?

I could answer neither question, but the mere fact that somebody had desired to buy, and had offered increasingly large sums for it, was a mighty important bit of information.

"I'll take a look at the fellow you've got under lock and key," Leverage was saying as he finished his third cup of coffee. "Maybe I'll recognize the scoundrel, and if so that ought to furnish a clew. Eh, Norton?"

"Undoubtedly," I replied. "You may be able to identify him."

"Won't hurt to have a look at him, at any rate," he went on. "And, since I have created all the destruction here that I can compass," he laughed, "suppose we take a look."

I arose. "Glad to exhibit him. Come right along. Tango has the key."

George and Rita remained where they were, and Leverage and I went below, Tango lighting the way for us. Blackhead looked up, a heavy scowl on his face, when we entered. Then, after his eyes grew accustomed to the light, he stared keenly at Leverage.

"Another damned cop, I suppose," he hazarded, after a short silence. "Well, cop or not, you won't get anything out of me. That's flat. Take yourselves out, if that's all you came for!"

"An impudent devil," Leverage commented, looking the prisoner over. "What was your idea, fellow, in impersonating Norton, and who hired you to? Answer those questions and maybe you won't fare so badly when things come to a head. What say?"

"Go to hell!"

"Oh, all right, if that's the way you look at it," Leverage returned, shrugging and turning to me. "I never saw the bird before. Hope you've got him chained good and tight, for if ever I saw an out-and-out villain, he's it. Let's go. I can breathe better out of here."

Tango led the way out, Leverage following, and I closed the door.

"Let me have the keys," I bade the negro. "Maybe I'd better have a look and make sure that chain is secure. Go ahead and show Mr. Leverage up. I'll use my flash."

Leverage turned, considered me for a moment, then went on toward the stairs with Tango. When certain I was alone, I swung the door open and sent the rays of my flash straight into Blackhead's face.

Just a hunch, maybe—but I played it.

The prisoner's wide mouth was sporting a grin, and he seemed immensely tickled over something. My return had not been anticipated, of course, and though he managed a heavy scowl almost on the instant the light was turned on his face, he had not been quick enough.

"Glad you are pleased with your quarters," I commented. "You'll need to be—for, contrary to your present belief, you're due to stay here for a good long while!"

I slammed the door and locked it—then pocketed the keys.

14

LEVERAGE GOES FISHING

I SOUGHT TANGO immediately after leaving the cellar, and found him in the back yard, talking to Paul Lemaitre. The Frenchman grinned, bowed courteously, and departed toward the lake.

"Tango," I said, approaching the negro, "I am taking it for granted that you are very fond of your Miss Rita. Am I right?"

His ivories showed in a broad grin. "Dat's right, suh!" he declared "En I ought to be. Wa'nt I theah when she war bawn? Sholy wuz. Lordy, when Miss Rita war a lil gal, she used to ride me eroun' th' place jes, lak I war a big, black mule! Haw-haw-haw! 'Clar' to goodness, suh, she did!"

"And you'd do anything in your power for her, I take it?"

His face sobered, and he gave me a level look. "Ah'd do anythin' suh, Whut does you-all want me to do?"

I started strolling slowly toward the open window of the morning room, my ears detecting voices of conversation there, and the negro followed.

"I'm going to be quite confidential with you, Tango," I said. "Miss Rita is in grave danger. There's a scoundrel who would kill her in cold blood, just to fill his pockets with money. He's not far off, either. He shot Mr. Roger Van, and has since tried to kill his children. I'm speaking of the fellow in the cellar. Are there any extra keys to those locks we've got on him and on the door?"

"Naw, suh," was his positive assurance. "Des dem whu's on dat ring you-all got in yo' pocket."

We were standing near the window of the morning room, having just reached it, and I raised my voice when I spoke again.

"I'm going to keep those keys, Tango," I informed him. "They'll stay in my pocket until this thing is over. When you feed him, I'll make it a point to be here. If I'm away, however, he'll just have to go hungry. That's flat."

I walked on, turned a corner of the house where I knew no one could observe me, and promptly thrust the ring of keys into the astonished darky's hand.

"Keep them, Tango!" I ordered, looking him squarely in the eyes. "Don't let anybody, even Miss Rita and Mr. George, know that you have them. Tell any one who asks, that I've got them. Understand? The safety of your mistress, and all of us, depends on it. You're safe just as long as it is believed that I have those keys—and no longer!"

"Cap'n, suh!" he gasped, his eyes rolling, "Ah doan rightly know whut all dis here is erbout—but ef anybody gits dese keys frum me, it'll be aftah Ah'm done daid! An' dat means eve'body!"

I walked into the house, thoroughly satisfied. Leverage was leaving the morning room as I entered the hall.

"Like to try for a bass or two?" he asked, pausing. "I'm going out for awhile. This is the season when they bite all day long. Hope they aren't laying off to-day."

"Some other time," I replied agreeably. "Got to pay a visit in the vicinity, so haven't time now. Good luck to you."

I passed into the morning room and immediately took George to task.

"Why didn't you tell me that somebody has been trying to dicker with you for Rockaway Place?" I demanded.

"Didn't think it important," he answered, surprised.

My young friend," I told him, "everything is important. Fortunately I learned this bit of news in time. How much was offered last time?"

"Two hundred thousand dollars," was the answer.

"So much? And what was the first offer, the first made your father?"

"Seventy-five thousand."

"W-he-e-ew-w-w—!" I whistled. "Somebody wants it bad! An increase of a hundred and twenty-five thousand! And you thought it unimportant! I'm disappointed in you, George—am, for a fact! By the way, I'm going to call on Friendly Joe right away, and while I'm gone you and Miss Rita remain in the house. Above all, don't venture out on the terrace, Upper or lower. I don't think the hillside harbors a killer to-day, but you never can tell. Promise?"

Both the Vans assured me they would obey, and I departed in search of a boat. At the landing I found Paul Lemaitre, but before I had a chance to engage him in conversation we were joined by Leverage, tackle-box and casting rod in hand.

"Better change your mind and go along," the sand dealer invited. "I've got an extra rod, if you want to use it."

"Sorry," I refused. "Got to call on a friend. See you later."

The fisherman departed, Lemaitre taking him in his boat. They headed up the lake. In a second boat I put off toward the south, having Friendly Joe's cabin boat in mind.

15

FRIENDLY JOE AS A HOST

WHEN I HAD gained the port side of the old hull which lay at anchor just short of the barrier at the lake's foot, I ceased rowing and looked the queer craft over.

The hull, what I could see of it, had been constructed out of hand-hewn boards, and how it kept afloat is more than I ever fathomed. From bow to stern it was probably twenty feet long, and measured some ten or twelve feet amidships. The superstructure was low, flat of roof, and built of odds and ends of boards, tin and saplings, the latter squared with an adz. Weather-stained and almost falling apart, the contraption was succumbing to age.

Having examined the craft, I hailed the skipper.

"Ahoy, on board the Wreck!" I shouted.

No answer came, nor did any one appear. "On board the Leviathan!" I bawled. "Maybe that name'll suit you better!"

No sign of recognition.

"Guess I'll just board her informally," I concluded, and laid my skiff alongside.

I had no more than set foot on deck when the cabin door opened and a gaunt scarecrow of a man loomed gigantically and frowningly before me. Clothed in odds and ends of raiment—doubtless supplied by the French population, since they are notoriously kindly toward those of unsound mind—he nevertheless was a dignified figure. His eyes were blue and faded, but I could imagine that they once sparkled with mighty fires. As for the rest of his features, they were almost concealed by a long, white beard. His hair, also white as snow, hung in a great, tangled cascade below his shoulders.

"What is your boat?" he demanded, his voice harsh.

"The Nemo, out of nowhere, cap'n," I answered glibly.

"You lie!" he cried fiercely. "The Nemo is at the bottom of the river! I saw her go down! Get off my boat!"

"Easy, Cap'n Joe," I begged soothingly. "I come to hold council with you—"

The old man's face underwent a sudden and complete change. A wide smile parted beard and mustache, betraying toothless gums. "Ah, Mr. Blake!" he exclaimed. "So you are back? Come right into the cabin. A better mate, sir, I confess a captain never had. I congratulate you, Mr. Blake, on the success of your mission. They are going to grant my request at last, I can see the news in your eyes! Good, Mr. Blake! Good!"

I hastened inside on the old man's heels, fearful that he might mistake me for somebody else and close the door before I could cross the threshold. He did not, however.

"You may be seated," he permitted gravely, motioning to a box beside a table. "Now, Mr. Blake, when is the United States Government going to put the Missouri back where she belongs, thus enabling me to complete my trip? The Blue Bell is long overdue, and I would be on my way."

"That's all right, cap'n," I assured him. "You won't have to wait long. Everything will be as you wish, never fear!"

"Will be! Will be! Will be!" he screamed suddenly, then broke into gust after gust of loud, croaking laughter. "Ah, Mr. Blake, we are very happy here!" he cried, after the merry mood had vanished. "We can depart whenever we wish. Hist!"

He tiptoed to the door, peered outside, then tottered over to a bunk. From beneath its covers he drew a long section of what appeared to be black rope—until closer inspection informed me as to its true character. A length of fuse, in fine.

"With this, and what goes with it," he said softly, a smirk on his toothless mouth, "we'll make our way. Never fear, Mr. Blake! Never fear!"

What the devil did the old loon mean, I wondered? Dynamite fuse. Where had he obtained it, and did he really have dynamite and caps?

Unlikely, I thought. Nobody, would bring in such to him, that was almost sure.

Suddenly the old man began to sing, at the top of his voice, old steamboat songs of an early day. He had seemingly forgotten me. The vocalizing kept up for a matter of five minutes, then the faded eyes were on me again.

"Why, Nelson, damn your hide!" he suddenly screamed. "You call yourself a pilot! A pilot! Ha-ha-ha-ha-ha! Ho-ho-ho-ho-ho! You couldn't steer a skiff through Dead Man's Chute without stoving her in, let alone a boat like the Blue Bell! Get off my deck, you—"

Then followed such a flow of sulphurous language as only a steamboat captain, and an oldtimer to boot, could have produced and aired. He rose, swinging his long arms about his head, and taking a poke at me every time he found himself within reach. The blows fell upon me without doing the least damage, and finally I gained the door, leaped into my boat and swung a lusty paddle away from there.

I'd learned all I wanted to know. Friendly Joe was the real stuff—a genuine lunatic. I was persuaded that his story would run substantially as it had been told by the natives—all except the millions of dollars' worth of silver bars. An injury to his head, at the time of the wreck, would account for his present mental condition. I have since had no reason for changing my opinion.

I had learned something else, too, while standing on the bow of old Joe's boat, looking down the valley which lay beneath the barrier. Something which would, as I had promised George, lift him off his feet when he should be informed of it.

Noon was at hand when I ascended the path to Rockaway House.

16

I PART WITH A FIFTY

I FOUND GEORGE in the library, his nose in a book.

"Have the Frenchies brought up any silver bars?" I asked quizzically. "There's a big fleet of small boats up the lake, and my glasses disclose much activity with drags and grab-hooks. They're on the job." George glanced up, tapping the open book with a finger. "I've been reading an old history of Missouri," he explained. "And it gives an account of the earthquake of which I told you. Mentions the loss of several steamboats, too. There was a boat called the Blue Bell, skippered by one Ben C. Barwick—Friendly Joe, no doubt. She has never been heard of since the quake. No mention is made of her cargo, however."

"Fine!" I applauded. "We'll all be rich maybe! Silver is bound to be found. Such labor now being expended in search of it, deserves success. In the meantime, answer a question:

"Why have you no dogs about?"

George frowned, and there was an angry note in his voice when he answered. "Somebody stole them!" he exclaimed. "We had two fine foxhounds—best in the country. One morning they got on the trail of a fox right here on the lawn, and followed it. They failed to return, and search has not recovered them. The only believable conclusion is that they trailed the quarry into the hills, and some thief, knowing their value, took them up."

"Too bad," I sympathized.

But George was wrong in the matter, I felt sure. I did not tell him what I thought about those dogs, because I did not want to make him uneasy. The explanation of the mystery involved, I thought, a member of his household—a servant.

Who?

Not Tango. The negro was true-blue, where his white folks were concerned.

Lemaitre?

Possibly. At any rate, I had a scheme for determining that point, and with that end in view I had George dig up the letter which he had written to me, and later received from Blackhead who stole it. Then I went upstairs to the room assigned me. It overlooked Lost Lake, and my glasses informed me that Uncle Frank was still casting for bass.

As for the incident of the dogs: A fox may have crossed the lawn of Rockaway House, but I thought it more likely that a bag of aniseed had been snaked across it, and that the picked carcasses of the hounds were at the moment lying beside the trail of the dummy fox—bullet-holes in their skulls.

That, at any rate, was how I doped it out.

I fell to examining the letter under a powerful reading-glass which I had picked up in the library. The flap of the envelope interested me.

"Lemaitre—just as I thought!"

Under the glass, the flap of the envelope disclosed positive proof that it had been sealed twice. The first time was, of course, with original mucilage, very light amber in color. The second sealing had been done with a heavier and darker glue.

Yes, the envelope had been tampered with, beyond doubt, which explains how my pursuers came to be on the trail in the cañon.

Next I examined the flap of the letter which I had sent to George. It also had been tampered with. Very neat had been the work done on the flaps of both envelopes—but the difference in the glue used to reseal them had given the thing away.

"Lemaitre," I repeated, "is the traitor. Doubtless the letter to me was opened and read in Black Pete's cabin, resealed and mailed. The answer received a like attention. Lemaitre, too, probably led the dogs off on a false scent, thus clearing the way in case it became necessary to prowl around down here and take close-range shots at the intended victims. All right, M. Lemaitre, we'll take care of you."

Somebody tapped on the door, and, in answer to my call, Tango came in.

"Mistah Petahs, suh," he announced, "done want to speechify wid you-all."

"Send him right in," I ordered, getting up.

"He done come erlong wid me," Tango replied, and Monkey showed up in the doorway.

"What's the news?" I inquired, after Tango had closed the door and gone.

"When you-all axed me erbout whar Slick Barzen—Dave, I means—done been stayin' since he got outen th' pen," the native said, "I had some sort of recollection erbout whut Pete said when he war at my cabin wunst. When I got home this mawnin', th' ole wumman remembered whut it was. So I come right over to let you-all know—an' git them fifty dollars."

"Spit it out," I ordered, reaching for my billbook. "The money is yours, if the news is worth it."

"Pete tol' us that Slick had a job as a special police-man, workin' fur a company, in Kansas City, which tuck sand outen th' river. Said he drawed good pay, an' didn't do nothin' to arn it, 'cept keep his eye out fur thieves on th' boats an' dredges. I reckon Pete knowed whut he war talkin' erbout."

Monkey Peters's news would have been cheap at any price, but fifty dollars is what he got.

"Here's the money," I said, thrusting the bill into his hand. "Now get out and put your nose to the ground again. Find out anything you can about Pete Barzen—when his funeral is to be, and all that. I'll see you later!"

Monkey departed, and I sat down to give matters a good, long thinking over. It was the dinner-call that aroused me.

Uncle Frank had had a bad day of it with the bass, it appeared, and was not in the best of humor. After Rita had withdrawn, he brought down a quart of prewar rye, intending to derive cheer from its contents. Of course, we were welcome to some cheer along with him.

"I never could stand much of that sort of stuff," I told him, after I'd downed a drink. "Sort of makes my head swim."

I took another, and told a funny story which I succeeded in mixing up so badly nobody laughed but me. It was such a funny story I was sorry they didn't get the point—and I drowned the sorrow in another snort.

By the time the bottle was half empty, George was looking at me with almost open contempt, and Uncle Frank's eyes had a queer expression when he turned them in my direction.

As for me, I forgot all about my companions—then awoke with a start. "Shleepy," I muttered thickly. "Sho dam shleepy, wanna go to bedsh!"

Uncle Frank motioned George to remain where he was. "I'll put him to bed," he said, grinning. "I see you are disgusted—and I don't blame you. No need for you to bother with him. Come, Norton!"

Uncle Frank undressed me, tenderly as a nurse would have an infant, and I was snoring drunkenly before he was out of the room.

But I didn't snore long. Half an hour later I got up like a thief in the night, and found my trousers. Then I locked the door securely, put a chair under the knob, and turned in for a real sleep.

A ring of keys was missing from my trousers' pocket. It had been there when I entered the room. Uncle Frank had undressed me.

Figure it out for yourself.

17

THE SEASON FOR SUCKERS

"**SLEEP WELL LAST** night, Norton?" Uncle Frank asked.

"Don't know whether I did or not," I grumbled. "I was asleep."

He grinned more broadly. "Tell you what's good for your malady this morning," he said suggestively. "A little of the hair of the dog that bit you."

"Waugh!" I choked, waving him away "Damn the stuff! I ain't used to it! Somebody had to put me to bed last night; Tango probably. I don't even remember! Never again!"

"That's what they all say!" he chuckled. "Well, go in and eat some breakfast, then you'll feel better. I'm off to tackle the bass again."

"Breakfast—not me!" I snapped. "Maybe I can hold a little black coffee, but I doubt it."

I was received coldly in the breakfast room. George and Rita were obviously displeased.

"Here are your keys, Mr. Norton," Rita told me, extending them toward me. "You must have dropped them out of your pocket last night."

I took the ring. "Just where did you find them?"

"On the floor beside the chair in which you sat," she replied.

"Thank you."

I drank my coffee in silence, and when George attempted to get me alone, obviously to voice his spleen, I evaded him.

"Got to go with Tango and feed Blackhead," I told him. "See you later. In the meantime—keep your shirt on!"

I didn't wait any longer, but routed Tango out and went below.

Barzen certainly was not smiling when we entered with the tray. His face was as black as a chunk of coal, and his eyes were bloodshot.

"Not feeling so well this morning, eh?" I gibed. "Got a terrible disappointment last night, didn't you? At about twelve o'clock, say, your heart beat high with hope—only to lower you into the black depths of despair, as the novelists say, a few minutes later. You heard some one fumbling the door-chain, a key querying a lock, then muttered oaths, footsteps receding—silence. What a shame! Want to talk?"

"Some day I mean to kill you!" he rapped.

"Ah, yes—some day," I taunted. "In some other world, possibly. Certainly not in this one—because you don't have a chance. As to your talking, I wouldn't listen if you did. Let me reconstruct.

"You left the pen and took a job, some time later, with Frank Leverage—a sort of pussy footer for his company. Later, you approached him with a scheme for making you both richer than double cream. You probably thought up the plan after listening to the babblings of Friendly Joe. Pete, who is dead now, by the way, may have originated it. At any rate, you and Leverage got together.

"Roger Van was killed; whether by you or Pete is of no moment, since you are an accessory and will swing anyhow.

Roger was killed because he would not sell out to Montgomery Nash. Nash, I am sure, would be amazed to learn that he had ever made an offer for the place. He didn't, as a matter of fact. His name was used by the fake real estate agent who made the offer, and had Roger accepted, another agent would have come forward immediately with an offer from you—or some other dummy for Leverage. A higher offer. That was the scheme. Nash was a stalking horse, so to speak.

"Roger wouldn't sell. He was killed. Maybe the heirs would part with the old rookery. But they wouldn't. All right, they, too, must be put out of the way. Two attempts were made, only to fail. Then I entered the case.

"No use to tell you about how Paul Lemaitre, loyal only to the highest bidder—Leverage, now—brought George Van's letter to you at Pete's cabin, and also allowed you a peep at my reply. You know all about it. You know, too, that Leverage came here yesterday morning, fully expecting to be greeted with the heart-breaking news of the mysterious killing of his niece and nephew. Why he failed to hear that news you already know.

"What you don't know is this: How I came to find out all your secrets. You'll know soon, however, so rest easy. Talk? You talk! Hell, you haven't anything new to tell me. Have you now?"

I left him staring after me with wide, startled eyes.

Upstairs, George made another effort to corner me, but I wasn't to be cornered. George would have to wait. I didn't dare let him know what I knew—unless I wanted to spoil one of the best cases in my experience. I therefore dodged him and went out on the lake—out where I could watch Uncle Frank, and his man Friday—alias Lemaitre.

When Leverage returned, late in the afternoon, he displayed a fine catch of bass, and seemed to be in better spirits than the day before. We ate the fish for supper—a silent supper, except for the efforts of the fisherman.

"Mr. Norton," said George, rising after the meal was over, "I wish to have a talk with you in the library."

"Sure!" I agreed. "Right after I have seen that Blackhead is fed, and safe for the night. Be with you in a shake!"

"I'll go along, if you don't mind," Leverage announced.

"Come along," I bade him.

"Directly after you return, Mr. Norton!" came the voice of George sharply, "It is very important!"

"Sure, George, I'll keep the date!" I returned as I left the room.

Tango led the way to the cellar and opened the door. Barzen sat up, and I thought his eyes were accusing when he recognized Leverage. In fact, I'm sure they were.

"Set the grub down, Tango," I ordered.

The negro, already schooled in his part, placed the tray on the floor near Barzen, then retired beside the door.

"A fine fried bass, that, Blackhead," I commented, pointing to one on the tray. "You must thank Mr. Leverage for it. He is the Walton who snared it. You sure have the dope right, Leverage," I complimented, turning to the fisherman. "It is the season for bass—and, I'll add, the season for suckers, too!"

And then I swung with all my force—a right to the point of Uncle Frank's jaw. He dropped with a grunt.

He hadn't come alive when Tango and I left the room—
after taking his gun from its holster—and locked the door.

"One more sucker in the net, Tango, old fellow, then
we'll have this case tied in a knot!" was my assurance to my
trusty aid as he climbed the stairs.

18

A DECEIVING CALM

GEORGE WAS WAITING for me in the library, and so was Rita. His eyes were hard; hers reproachful.

"I'm afraid we can't depend on you, Mr. Norton," George said coldly. "Last night's performance was, to say the least for it, disappointing. Illuminating as well—"

"Just a moment, Mr. Van," I interrupted, looking him squarely in the eyes. "You, like your two foxhounds, are off on a false scent. It suited me to act in such a manner, last evening, so as to convince a certain person that I was stupefied with liquor. It was very important that he should believe that." I turned to Rita. "Those keys you found on the dining room floor were not left there by me. They were stolen out of my pocket while I, presumably, lay helpless in a drunken sleep. They were not, however, the keys wanted—just a bit of rat-bait, so to speak. Disappointed, the purloiner dropped them in the dining room this morning, the inference being that I had lost them there."

"I regret that it was necessary to keep you in the dark, both of you," I assured them, "but it couldn't be helped. You will understand that when the matter is made clear to you. I can promise that this case will be concluded by

to-morrow morning, and at an early hour. Does my explanation satisfy you?"

George's face had gradually cleared, as my explanation
developed. At its end, he unbent.

"You acted very drunk, I must say," he remarked. "Took
me in, and I'm sure Uncle Frank was deceived too."

"Yes," I agreed. "Uncle Frank was deceived. That, too,
couldn't be helped. Believe me, though, Uncle Frank's
respect for my cold-sober mentality is rising by leaps and
bounds at this moment. Of that you may be assured."

"Oh," Rita exclaimed, pleased, "you have explained the
matter to him?"

I nodded. "He understands—perfectly."

"Sorry for the misunderstanding," George apologized.
"Though, as a fact, you have yourself to blame."

"I accept it," I replied. "Now for a smoke, then a stroll
in the moonlight along the bluffs. I've got a bit of thinking to do."

When I returned to the house, an hour later, and entered
the drawing-room, Rita met me with a question:

"Where is Uncle Frank, Mr. Norton? Do you know?"

"I clear forgot to tell you!" I exclaimed contritely. "When
we came up from feeding Blackhead, Leverage went to his
room. Said he was tired, and was suffering from, er—the
toothache, I believe it was. Meant to go to bed at once."

"Oh, then, I must go up and see how he is!" Rita
exclaimed, starting.

"I wouldn't," I admonished. "He expressly said to tell
you and George not to disturb him. He would be all right
after a good sleep, he thought."

Rita returned to her book, and, bidding them good

night, I went upstairs. The night, I felt sure, would prove uneventful. I could go to sleep with the consciousness of work well done. I had only to await the coming of morning, and with it the other "sucker."

Lemaitre. He always reported just after dawn, being employed by the Vans chiefly to run errands to and from Kirkland, and watch for forest fires. He would come—but would not go away again until the time came to take him out to jail.

The case was settled. Sure I'd sleep.

But I didn't. Couldn't make up my mind to go to bed. A sort of restlessness laid hold on me, and I finally went back to the bluffs, to smoke a pipe and watch the moonlit water. After the excitement of the past two days, the calm which had settled over me was irksome. Too extreme. A pipe would quiet me and soothe me inside—like the surface of Lac le Noir, which lay like sheet glass, without the slightest motion.

Yes, it was calm. A deceitful calm, like that supposed to precede a tornado.

A deep, hollow groan of agony, coming from the shadows near the trail down to the beach, smote on my ears—and the tornado was in motion!

19

ON THE CELLAR STAIRS

A TRAP?

I dismissed the thought, and the next moment was bending over a bloody figure beside the path. It was Tango.

"Cap'n No'tun, suh!" he gasped, when I had lifted his head and made him understand who I was, "dem keys—is—gone! He tuck—'em!"

"Who?" I demanded. "Tell me who, Tango?"

"He cum to—my do', lil while—ago, an' said dat you-all wanted—me quick, down on de beach. I went out to fin' whar at you waz, an' den—wham! On mah—haid! Den—I doan know—nuffin', 'cept de—keys is—gone!"

"Who got them?" I pleaded. "Quick—"

"Dat Paul Lemattah—"

I waited for no more. The front door was open, having been left so by me, and I reached the hall in less time than it requires to tell about it. There, in the darkness, I paused to consider.

How long had Lemaitre had those keys in his possession? Had he already effected the release of Barzen and Leverage? If so, what was going on in those upper rooms—Rita's and George's rooms?

I shivered.

Then I took courage. They would not dare harm the Vans until I was out of the way. With me dead, they could dispose of the other two in comparative safety. But, with me alive, they would be afraid to proceed, as I might, for all their precautions, escape and hang them for their crimes.

That conclusion gave me heart. I listened intently, but could detect no sound from above. Then I crept to the cellar door and opened it cautiously. Thank God there was only one entrance!

No sound came from that dark hole, and I stole down the stairs, one step at a time, my flash in readiness to flood the place with light, and my gun in hand. About half way down I stopped, leaned against the balustrade and peered through the blackness toward the door behind which my captives had been.

Not a sound, not a glimmer of light rewarded me. Had they escaped clear of the premises?

That thought was answered immediately. They had not. They would not leave until after doing all in their power to kill me, at least. For I held their lives in my hands.

Suddenly my ears caught the sound of a chain being rattled, ever so faintly, then a thin pencil of light showed me an open door—and in the door stood Leverage, peering out, a pistol gripped in his hand.

The light went out, and I crouched lower in the protection of the balustrade. A mutter of voices came to my ears, followed by an indistinct rustle as of feet searching along the dark floor. I waited.

Presently the shuffling came nearer—nearer—

I leaped up, sent a shaft of blinding light from my flash

stabbing through the blackness—and a slug from my gun a split second later.

A sharp cry followed the deafening explosion of my powder, and I ducked to cover in time to avoid the bullets which sang over me and buried themselves in the wall.

What would happen next? What move would they make?

I heard a groan, a gurgling cry, and the sound of boot heels beating a tattoo on the floor—then silence.

Who had I killed? Leverage, Barzen, or Lemaitre?

Would not George and Rita be aroused by the gunfire, and come on the scene, probably bringing lights? That possibility sent me craw-fishing up the stairs. They must be halted at any cost.

Reaching the door, I pushed it open, backed into the hall—and came squarely against some one who was in the act of entering the cellarway. A pair of arms encircled me.

"No you doan!" rasped a voice. "Ah done cotch you—"

"Tango!" I whispered. "It's me—Norton!"

"Godalmighty!" he gasped, releasing me. "Ah thought they done kilt you! "

Wham!

A gun roared at the foot of the stairs, and a bullet snarled by us. I leaped aside, dragging Tango with me, and thrust one of my guns into his hand. The next moment the stairway shook under the charge of those below, and a steady stream of lead poured into the hall. The passageway down into that cellar might have been likened to a popping machine gun nest.

"They're rushing us!" I cried to Tango, just as a shrill scream sounded from the floor above.

"Norton! Norton!" shouted George from the stairhead.

"Stay where you are!" I shouted. "Get ready to shoot, Tango!"

I pressed the button on my flash and flooded the cellarway with light, just as a frightful figure, six-gun blazing, burst through. I swung my gun on him and let drive.

Leverage, for it was he, crashed down—and his fall was all that saved Barzen, directly behind him, from getting Tango's bullet through the chest. Barzen tripped over the prostrate Leverage, and the bullet entered his throat instead.

The next instant Rita, in her nightdress, ran downstairs into the hall. George, a gun in hand, came behind her.

"Go back!" I ordered. "Take her back, George—this is no sight for her!"

Then she saw that bloody heap in the doorway, with Barzen squirming on top—and fainted.

"See to Barzen!" I called to Tango, and leaped to pick up the still form of the girl.

Then, with a roar which surpassed any like sound that ever greeted my ears, the universe seemed to explode. The big house shook and rocked, pictures fell from the walls, furniture leaped from the floor and went skidding against the walls—and I found myself on my knees, shaken beyond the power of speech, even of thought!

20

ROLLING WATERS

THE TERRIFIC CONCUSSION ceased as abruptly as it had begun. Forgetting all about Barzen, I staggered up and dashed outside—followed by George, with Rita, whom the disturbance had revived, caught in his strong arms. Tango, streaming blood from a wounded head, was on our heels.

With one accord we turned toward the lake—why, I had never tried to explain even to myself. Instinct, call it. When we stood on the bluff we gradually came to comprehend what had happened.

The moon gave a light almost like day, and, to our astonishment, we saw that the surface of the lake was below its usual level and receding rapidly. It surged southward, impelled by a fierce current!

A long glance to the south—and the whole thing dawned upon me.

"There's the answer to the problem, George!" I exclaimed. "The solution to the mystery I came to solve! I knew about it yesterday, but feared you would not believe it!

"Friendly Joe grew tired of waiting for the government to restore the river, so he could take the Blue Bell on to her journey's end—so he shot that barrier at the foot of the lake with a tremendous charge of dynamite! He hinted as much yesterday! See, the barrier is gone, the lake pouring its flood into the valley below—a valley which is, in reality, but the old bed of the Missouri. Joe has made his last run!

"See what that means to you? No railroad could come here and confer value on the coal—and now none is needed. There is a vastly easier way, and a far cheaper one. Don't you understand? A lock and dam at the mouth of the stream now forming, flung across it where it joins the Missouri, with the flow of those springs ever swelling the tide, there'll be a natural waterway from here clear to Kansas City—the greatest coal-distributing center in all the West! Now do you get it?"

"I do!" cried George, white and shaken. "But what had this to do with the killing of father, and the attempts on us?"

Then, as gently as I could, I broke the news.

"Leverage saw the possibilities the moment Barzen called his attention to what could be done with the dam, and the prospects of possessing such a stupendously valuable property swept away any honor he may have had, likewise any affection for you and Rita, which could not have been very deep at best. He yielded. Went away to Europe, presumably, and waited until the news reached him that Roger was dead. Then he came back, hoping to get you to sell. You wouldn't, and it was, therefore, on the cards that you should die.

"Leverage looked like a promising suspect the moment I learned that he would inherit in case you and Rita died intestate—and, from his viewpoint, even if you made wills. He was the only near kin, and you both were fond of him.

But what caused me to connect him strongly in my mind was this:

"When I saw him coming up the path that first morning, it was not he alone whom I saw. I saw his steam tugs, barges—his sand-dredging activities, in fine. It immediately popped into my mind that this property would be immensely valuable for its coal, provided the coal could be transported to Kansas City by water. When I saw that the valley below the dam was a direct outlet to the Missouri, I had my case complete.

"Leverage stole my keys in order to free his man Barzen, after which he meant to kill you and Rita, and me, of course, and let it be thought that the prisoner escaped and did it. Barzen, of course, would then have had to make himself scarce—but he would have had to do that in any case, because he was already known to be in it up to his neck.

"When your uncle learned that the keys he stole were only my office keys, he immediately suspected a trick. Lemaitre got orders to waylay Tango and search him for them. The Frenchman got the keys, and went at once to liberate Barzen, taking arms with him. He was, no doubt, astonished to find Leverage also a prisoner.

"That's the history of the whole case, as I see it, and I believe that it is materially correct."

I honestly believe that if Barzen had not told it all before he died, those two young folks would never have believed fully in their uncle's perfidy. But he did.

"It was just like you said in the cellar," he told me, just before he succumbed to the wound in the neck. "I heard Old Joe talking about the lake going back to the river, should he blow the dam out of the way—and I got the idea. Leverage would inherit, if the Vans were out of the way. We tried to buy, but they wouldn't sell—and that's all there is to say. Maybe, though, I'd better tell you that I shot Roger Van. Pete was the one that killed the dogs, and tried to kill the boy.

"Oh, yes," he went on, his voice growing weak, "I want to tell you, damn you, that I'm lying here dying all because I listened to Pete. I saw you still was living there in the cañon, and wanted to finish you. But Pete said he'd rather not do it so close to his cabin, and that if you came round he'd make you walk to your death in the river. Hadn't been for that, Pete would be alive— But, oh hell! What's the use!"

He died a few minutes later.

THE INCIDENTS HEREIN related were recalled to me very vividly the other day—hence the story. I was standing at my office window, which commands a fine view of the Missouri, and my glance dwelled upon an important little steam tug—the tug Norton, named for me. It was towing half a dozen laden barges. George's and Rita's coal, pouring in from their colossal mine!

.

www.ingramcontent.com/pod-product-compliance
Lightning Source LLC
Chambersburg PA
CBHW031213020726
47499CB00002B/564